NEW   EM

HARBOR LIGHTS

HARBOR LIGHTS

A NOVEL

THEODORE WEESNER

Atlantic Monthly Press
New York

Published simultaneously in Canada
Printed in the United States of America

FIRST EDITION

Library of Congress Cataloging-in-Publication Data
Weesner, Theodore.
    Harbor lights : a novel / Theodore Weesner.
        p.   cm.
    ISBN 0-87113-766-6
    I. Title.
    PS3573.E36H37   2000
    813'.54—dc21   99-29863
                                                        CIP

Design by Laura Hammond Hough

Atlantic Monthly Press
841 Broadway
New York, NY 10003

00 01 02 03   10 9 8 7 6 5 4 3 2 1

The same old harbor lights . . .
that once brought you to me.
Jimmy Kennedy, 1937

ONE

WARREN

He turned his lobster boat upstream and gave her some speed, though not much. She was a '48 Jonesporter, a thirty-two footer, and she rode low in the stern and high in the bow. Her hull had been refinished yearly with fiberglass quality bottom paint, and in her lifetime her structure and pilothouse had been stripped and repainted eleven times. She remained a handsome boat and one of the oldest in service though decay was setting in with her, as it was with her owner, and Warren knew they both were doomed.

Seas were placid and it was unseasonably warm for October. The pastures of harbor water were as thinly green as old mirrors, with fissures of air escaping fault lines here and there as if hissed from whales. Fishing boats passed soundlessly in the distance, and all around was the solitude that came with the livelihood of one man hauling traps within sight of land. Larger boats carrying radar and crews went far out and stayed weeks at a time, but were neither as solitary nor as philosophical as the one-man entities.

Lobstering and independence went hand in hand. Within a hundred yards of shore were depths over forty

4

THEODORETHEODORE WEESNER

fathoms, and within the volume of black water along reefs and seaweed-draped valleys lay promises of treasure in forms of fish and crustacea, together with daily threats of death and discouragement. Questions were ever present for lobstermen: Can you stand the loneliness? What of the cold water on your hands, the smell of bait in your lungs and rowing out before dawn in snow squalls, pouring rain, uncompromising walls of wind? What of your oilskins getting tangled and finding yourself pulled over the side? What of the times when lobsters aren't feeding, or when a glut is on the market? And your family—will they provide the support on land a lobsterman needs to succeed at sea? Why not trade some of that mean independence for a seat at the wheel of a backhoe, for wages, regular hours, the camaraderie of a factory with dry wooden floors, heated air, a candy machine? For coffee and talk with friends . . . at least until a foreman came cracking the whip?

Why not trade the whole wet, risky business—as Warren had for eight years, not that long ago—for a civil service rating with the State Water Pollution Commission? Yes, for rancorous disputes with neighbors over lab readings and subsurface disposal pollutants. Yes, for that brown cap and labeled jacket he had been ashamed to wear in the presence of his wife, however rarely she looked his way.

Through no wish of his own Warren was coming in early today and had the *Lady Bee* riding an incoming tide at minimum power. All about was calm as the boat sliced a quiet V and, resting against his jerry-built driver's seat, he gazed within as he kept the boat on course. He strove to be as even-tempered as the day itself and to keep his thoughts under control. For he was fifty-seven, his cough had grown chronic, and the threat of mortality had been intercepting his view for a string of months. He gazed into the breach now as the hull slapped the water like an opened hand and sent a spattering over the windshield and one side of his face. He couldn't help thinking how satisfying it would be to motor forever into the Indian summer horizon. What a dream it would be to pursue the horizon and leave his problems washing away in the suds.

He'd have to talk to Beatrice soon and explain what was happening. Her blatant affair had been hard to believe but he had lived with it all these years and it was a fact of life. If there was a saving grace it was that they lived in the same house, if not entirely as husband and wife, and saw each other, spoke to each other two or three times a week. Now this turn in the road—if his lungs proved malignant, as he knew they would. The thought of her living on, and of Virgil Pound being ever in her midst, touching her, lying in bed with her, set off Warren's lifetime of resentment every time he thought of it.

Dear Beatrice. Nearly all his life Warren had had thoughts of hurting her for the pain she had made him suffer. The thoughts surfaced as if on their own, though he never allowed them serious entry into his mind. Shooting, stabbing, choking. Suppressed fantasies of forcing her to submit. Compelling her to lower to her knees, to remove her clothes. Still, when the fantasies tried for center stage, he pulled a curtain down on his mind. He had gained some wisdom with age, and violating her was nothing he wanted to have on his conscience. Not with so little time left. She may have treated him badly but he wouldn't be returning the favor. Taking the high road, at this time in his life, had become his only hope for peace of mind.

Warren had a string of traps just ahead and wasn't sure he would run them, though habit would make stopping hard to resist. Turning from traps along Outer South Banke was one thing, but crossing the harbor to Narrow Cove and motoring by a last string would be like passing his own child on the highway and looking ahead as if he hadn't seen her.

His strings held six traps each and were marked by buoys at each end plus a toggle buoy for each trap. Like charms on a Krylon bracelet, the traps lay where they settled on the bottom, and their locations would be changed if they failed to produce. When they produced well, when they fell not to lifeless muck but into lobster playgrounds and tenements within rocks and kelp, attempts were made to return them over and over to the same locations.

Throughout the years Warren had maintained fifty to seventy strings, three to four hundred traps in all, but had had difficulty in recent years keeping up with twenty strings, running half daily in the high season and exhausting himself doing so. Working ever more slowly, he had to pause, gasp, and gather strength to raise, clear, rebait, and return a plastic-coated wire trap to the cold, sloshing water. His grounds—a 700-yard stretch along Outer South Banke, twenty acres of seaweed-draped ledges and rocky valleys, plus the two-acre spit there in Narrow Cove, near where he moored his boat—had been his father's grounds and mooring site before him and were his as if legally deeded. If another fisherman, or a ragpicker—some airline pilot or professor wanting to impress visitors with a crate of lobsters for dinner—put out traps in a lobsterman's area, the intruder would be subjected to a warning and the surrendering of his catch or, more likely, to having his trap lines cut in his absence. Remaining obstinate, an interloper could count on having his boat cut loose in the dead of night, even introduced to some bullet holes and the havoc a half-sunken vessel left behind, though instances of lobstermen using rifles and pistols were rare. Warren knew of maybe six boats burned or put on the bottom over four decades and but three armed assaults, each an occasion of a ragpicker insisting on keeping a catch he'd taken and needing the crack of a rifle close to the hull to see that no matter legal niceties a lobsterman's grounds were not subject to negotiation.

Narrow Cove, northwest between Gerrish Island and the mainland, was coming into view and Warren had to decide whether to pull his last string or move on to the Co-op with what he had—an embarrassing half-dozen three-quarter pounders. The last string represented the call of duty, of being a highliner rather than a dub in the community of lobstermen. Creatures in traps would survive weeks without being harvested, but their lives were finite and crowded traps were inhospitable to newcomers. Lobsters and crabs cannibalized in fights to the death, and the tables had to be reset twice or more a week in season if a profit was to be realized.

There came one of Warren's familiar green-and-white striped buoys breaking the surface and, helpless against the old pull, he cut the *Lady Bee*'s engine to neutral and let her sink-belly toward the bobbing pin with its balancing stick. He had accumulated some strength by then and proceeded to work slowly and one step at a time. He used a metal hook to snare the line and lifted the rope to within reach of his left hand. He had not given in to coughing, though he was expending breath and strength rapidly, and he held for the moment against the rising and falling of his broad thirty-foot boat. Seas remained calm, but for the waves he'd created. Bent close to the chilled water, hands wet, the air temperature had to be in the 60s, and the warm October day was growing warmer and more thought-provoking. The American League play-offs were under way—in New York or Baltimore, he wasn't sure—and for a moment he glimpsed himself in the solitary long-ago, when baseball had been an afternoon more than an evening game and his summertime work on swaying salt water had been joined by announcers narrating balls and strikes, hits and runs from Fenway Park in Boston, just fifty miles south by southwest by way of the sea.

Sensing an accumulated body of strength, he readied for the next step. Okay, he told himself and, reaching a rubber-gloved hand to grip the rope, backed off half a step, lifted the dripping line with both hands, and placed it on the snatch block he had long ago connected to the *Lady Bee*'s hydraulic hauler and straight-six Chevy engine.

He paused again, gathering added breath and strength. No breeze was moving over the water, leaving the pastures free of ripples, and he knew it was one of those days when people on land would be using terms like glorious and gorgeous, and conniving to be out in the intoxicating air. Well, at least he'd had an outdoor life to both endure and enjoy, he thought. Every day he had tasted air and sky; his pipe and cigarette smoking may have diluted taking in the elements, but even that combination had been satisfying until the time came, some months back, to commence paying the tobacco piper.

He continued to pause and, staring once more over the horizon, still did not push the button that in its engaging of the wheel would bring line and seawater spinning and, in a moment, the first trap breaking the surface and draining in a rush. How could any wife do to a husband what she had done to him? Why had he settled into living with her infidelity when he could have made another life for himself?

Rested, suppressing his coughing with his fist, Warren managed for the moment to glimpse the bounty of the sea and the anticipation which had thrilled him from the first time, as a seven-year-old, he hoisted a trap to the light of day. The thrill of fishing—you never knew what a trap might contain: A five-pounder the size of a first baseman's glove? A three-foot sand shark thrashing within the cage? Five or six three-pounders in one trap, as in his father's stories? An albino to deliver to the fish biologists upstream at the university's Great Bay Estuarine Lab—or maybe a four-inch-thick flounder to take home and slice into filets for dinner and the freezer? The unknown sea. He had pulled traps all his life, and here in the bottom of the ninth its eternal appeal had only grown deeper and more mysterious.

The *Lady Bee* kept putting up bubbles in neutral and, line in hand, holding his own against the pull between boat and water, Warren proceeded to the first trap. The *Lady Bee*'s hauler was positioned at the widest part of the boat's pumpkin seed shape and, taking in a breath, he pressed the button that started rope and salt water spinning. Subconsciously measuring time, he watched for the wire mesh to break through, ready to hit the clutch and bring the trap to rest on the railing.

The small climax occurred in a rush of water and there followed the old disappointment of scanning the contents: Some crabs and three undersized juveniles, a seeder loaded with eggs, maybe one keeper. His thought at the moment was that all he had ever wanted was to have her as his wife and to be a good husband and that his inability to do so was a splinter in his heart he was trying yet to accommodate. Now this stupid cancer, sending tentacles into his lungs and throat. If there was a God in heaven—as he had been taught to believe—what kind of justice was this for a man already cheated by life for thirty years?

Exhaling small breaths, Warren began processing the catch, tossing back crabs and juveniles. Lifting the seeder by her carapace—confirming that her tail was notched, probably by him—he settled her to the surface on her back that she might cascade into the deep and not lose eggs by being thrown. Returning seeders was the law of lobstering, that fishing might proceed indefinitely. Warren knew all about nurturing the sea and about life being unfair, and this latest blow to his well-being kept coming up anew. Where to from here? How could he get through to her with this added clock ticking in his ear?

BEATRICE

At home on Kittery Point she was getting ready for work. A woman of independent means, she ran her own store and her morning routine was one of charging herself like a battery for the day. She liked kidding with herself through-out the process, but had her routine down and meant to leave the house looking good and feeling right. Each day was a minor struggle, however insignificant the obstacles might appear to others to be. Being a woman was ob-stacle number one, Beatrice thought, and maybe one through ten. Did men have any idea of the games women had to play?

Leaning to her bedroom mirror, Beatrice upflapped her chin with her fingers, all for naught, she imagined. She slapped her modest thighs and, over her shoulder, tried for a view of a butt some might say was pretty cute for a fifty-five-year-old but which seemed to her to be on an eternal mission to smother any seat with which it came into contact. Staying pretty and a little sexy was a full-time job in itself, and stepping from the mirror for a more detached view, she said to herself, *Come on, you're not so bad. Just be vigilant. Think of the blubber and wrinkles*

that overwhelm so many. No sweets, sauces, rationaliza-
tions. Think how your chin will sag if you let them have
their way! Be vigilant! Savor vegetables! Savor sweat! Thus
Beatrice's version of a morning pep talk—motivating herself to be in charge of her self and the day.

Extracting a silk kerchief from her scarf drawer, she
stuck it in the breast pocket of a camel's hair blazer she
had placed on her wooden dressing tree. The weightless
kerchief added a flair she wanted—autumn leaves on a
field of beige—and the walnut dressing tree was an En-
glish import she used each morning as a prop in preparing her schedule. Skirt, blouse, shoes. Appointments and
calls. Revisions were easy: brighter shoes, lighter blouse,
wider belt. Something a little French or, if sun and season were right—as they appeared to be today—a touch
of Vermont with its colors peaking. A steady smile to off-
set her sinking old face—if only the steady smile did not
begin to hurt after two minutes.

The kerchief helped, and her spirits were getting on
track. Just before daybreak she had suffered another guilt
dream, but now she felt high-spirited, a sensation that had
been surfacing often lately. Was it dues paid, or a product of growing older? She *felt* young, in any case, and not
clueless but the best kind of young: aware. She had only
to remain vigilant in diet and outlook, in taking care of
business. *Keep going forward,* she told herself. *Don't let*
the past drag you down like barnacles on a boat.

Sometimes Beatrice made her wardrobe selections the night before and positioned an outfit and shoes on the way to bed—one of the acts her daughter, Marian, called her "Martha Stewart gene." Then, in the morning, sipping coffee and making up, as she was doing now, she considered the outfit and once more previewed her day's agenda. (Scandia rep at three, Windows tutorial at four, but mainly, at ten this morning, a coffee "talk" at a local business college that—let's face it—had dominated her thoughts all week. Then lunch as usual with Virgil, and, finally, ad copy dropped off at the *Herald* before five. A coming and going day. An okay day, once she got through giving that talk, the thought of which kept making her seem to float with stage fright.)

Red shoes? She imagined the business school girls being fun and wanted her outfit to convey a mix of quality and pizzazz, independence and femininity—something to express the person she had long been struggling to be. If she could have them thinking "that's how I want to be when I'm her age," anything else they got from her would be gravy.

Studying a rack of shoes, she was wondering if Marian, who was now twenty-seven, would gain similar fulfillment in her life or if she would be handicapped for having grown up approximately happy? Beatrice worried at times that Marian had had things too easy and might prove short in grit over the long haul. What good was a legacy if your kid

flopped at forty and had forty years yet to go? Early disappointment could prove ultimately creative; it was something
she had used like fuel to drive herself, while Marian—an
only child—had grown up more prosperous than most and
had escaped, really, being inhibited by her father's old-
fashioned and possessive manner.

Beatrice thought again that she could write a book
about ultimate creativity. Wouldn't that be something? The
secret was that while everything had a price the payments
could be turned into fuel; the method lay in converting
burdens and never forgetting where the power was coming from. Wouldn't writing a book be something? That
business school wouldn't be inviting her for a coffee klatch,
they'd be asking her to be a professor!

Oh, you're the ticket all right, she told herself, *now
get it moving.*

The ringing phone stabbed Beatrice's train of thought like
an omen in an old movie. Just as she was leaving, the
phone rang once and stopped; its sound reminded her
how quiet it was in the house and though she dismissed
the ringing as a misdialing, it threw her off for a moment.
The sound raised in her the unpleasant sensation of having
dreamt of Warren. Her dreams of him followed a pattern:
Bizarre narratives would raise guilt to a near-breaking pitch
(that morning they had been in an open-air kitchen on a
dock surrounded by high water, gulls, white yachts) only

to have the sensation outdone by a greater horror of re-submitting to his authority, as in their first years of marriage. She awakened to a hammering heart and here, being stabbed by the phone on leaving the house, her heart was pounding again. Shake it off, she thought. Dreams are for venting, not for altering behavior.

Trying to envision her business card (imagining confiding to the business school girls how much she loved the modest little token of self-worth!), Beatrice had to jam her brakes when a dirty blue Toyota stopped short before her. There—as offensive as Warren in her dream—was the filthy car throughout the light cycle and was the impulse for her turning left, toward Jiffy Car Wash (she had time) rather than right to the Kittery Mall and her store.

Another thought was on her mind: The college girls would see her pull in and park and would be impressed by her sparkling red LeBaron. That, and a prevailing thought: She needed to add her daughter's name to her new batch of business cards, just as she wanted Marian to add her name to her own. It's good PR, she'd explain to Marian when she came in. A mother and daughter in business together was something people would *like*. A small thing, but one of those small things that added up. Wouldn't *she* like it if she were a potential customer? Say you're undecided between a chain outlet like Pier I and a shop co-owned by a mother and daughter—where would you go? She could tell her where she'd go and it sure wouldn't be to some franchise stamped out with a cookie cutter! Beatrice anticipated getting a chortle from Virgil if she dropped the image at lunch. He enjoyed teasing her over her devotion to the store, and like a schoolgirl being teased over a boyfriend it made her glow with pleasure every time.

Returning north to the Mall, car glistening and dripping, she wondered again why the day had such a promising feel and, buzzing her window down, realized what it was: The air was oddly warm and aromatic. Blue skies and sunlight were reflecting within an aroma that reminded her of Southern California at daybreak—an experience she and Virgil had shared on a getaway trip a couple years ago that not even Marian had learned about. Air off the Pacific had carried a warm scent of ocean, rose hips, wine, a California scent of exalted dreams and one she had not thought of in months.

She buzzed the window down all the way, like a teenager. Yeah, grand day for singing, Marian would say, some such droll nonsense, and they'd laugh and feel wonderful over being mother and daughter. What a blessing to have a daughter and to be in business together! Could anyone be luckier than she had turned out to be—if luck, she thought, had been the half of it? For she was in love with life now, that was the bottom line, even if that dark shadow continued to trail along. She was in love with her work, in love with her daughter, in love with the future. And now that Virgil was retired from office, who knew, maybe they'd shake things up a bit. Though what she fantasized about most was being celebrated in time by Marian and the children Marian wanted to have. In her fantasy they toasted her as the one who had started it all, who had made their lives complete. She only hoped they would gain half the satisfaction in what she left behind as she was knowing in its making. It wouldn't be a smelly blood and guts enterprise, that was for sure, though, heaven knew, Warren hadn't lacked initiative so much as he had lacked flair. How sad his life had been; it constricted her heart to think of it—as she was doing just then, turning in at the Mall—and she told it and him yet again to leave her alone, to invade someone else's thoughts.

He wouldn't have listened to reason anyway, and who could say his life would have been any better had she been a nice little fisherman's wife who talked to him by CB every time he was out on the water? The disdain he felt for her store and the years she had given to it—he had no idea, really, of the fulfillment an independent business could bring. He who had boat, traps, fishing rights handed to him by his father—had he been so independent? One thing was certain: However he spoke of his boat he did not understand the companionship she derived from her business. For the store was all but alive and moved with her day in and day out. Virgil understood.

He knew that it was her passion and would smile and know just where she was coming from if she said something about the companionship of inventory, showcases, new orders. But even Virgil would be surprised at the depth of her devotion. For with the exception of her daughter, nothing or no one had become a closer companion to her than her store, its floor and aisles, its merchandise, the customers. To be there in the evening after closing, on Sunday morning before opening, to straighten (again) misplaced candle holders and salt and pepper shakers. For her it was like touching back a strand of Marian's hair when she was a child, or straightening her collar today, picking a piece of lint from her lapel and smiling, to have her know she loved her.

Pleased (again, deeply) that her life included a parking space, Beatrice nosed in the glistening red LeBaron and turned off the engine. Check and double-check. Lights. Windows. 08:27. Disappointed that Marian had yet to arrive—they didn't open until ten but she had made it clear to her daughter that nine was managerial starting time— Beatrice gathered her purse and leather portfolio and unfolded into the unusual warmth of the days.

Southern California along the coast of Maine—sea air and aroma in a crossing of stars and planets. As in all the songs, the day was evoking fantasies in her youthful-feeling heart. Let's close this place and go to the beach,

Marian would joke, but this morning she might just beat her to the punch with some such remark, Beatrice was thinking. She smiled in anticipation as she bypassed the rear fire exit, heading around to the main entrance. She readied her keys as she walked; just before her, behind twin locks in the glistening plate glass doorway, was her home away from home, her world of dreams.

MARIAN

She paused at the bottom of the stairs. Listening, she heard nothing. No movement, no water running. "Ron?" she said. Her mind traveled somewhere, she knew not where, and as she returned she still heard nothing. "Ron, it's after eight."

Back in the kitchen, rinsing her cup, it came to Marian how regularly she was alone with herself and how it was a state she had come to prefer. Overhead, the toilet flushed. Any minute Ron would clomp downstairs grumbling, and it also came to her that his arrivals had begun to interfere with her being alone with herself, rather than being small filial fulfillments. Secretly pregnant, two plus months along, she let her belly touch over the rim of the sink before her. *Mon petit bijou,* her lips allowed in endearment to her secret child. A baby. A new person to grow up and be—a new person with a new life! Ron might go postal when he heard the news but she didn't care;

the thrill it was giving her had to be the sweetest she had ever known.

He passed behind her, going to the coffeepot, and she sensed again the interruption of her private universe. Say something nice, she thought of her husband, as if to allow him a chance to redeem himself. But by the time she finished at the sink and turned his way he had said nothing at all.

"Hey, good morning," she said.

"Hey."

He was reading their home-delivered *Globe* and Marian, wondering yet again how to get him told of their impending addition, decided it was not the time and moved toward the stairs. Always she said something of having to shower, get dressed, leave for work, but she decided here, in the superior and surreal status of herself as a mother-to-be, to say nothing at all.

"Hh—Marian," she heard as she began climbing the stairs.

"Have to get dressed, I'm running late," she said.

"Hh," she heard and knew he hadn't missed a word in whatever he was reading.

In the bathroom, getting naked as shower water heated, Marian took a look at her profile in the mirror. Not now but one day in May she would resemble Demi Moore in *Vanity Fair*, one hand resting on her expanded belly. For now there was but the merest sign at her midsection—well, no sign at all unless she imagined a vague expansion there. Ron. Maybe it would be fun to share nonsensical pregnancy thoughts with him, but it was also fun to leave him in the dark and keep them to herself. In truth, well, he wasn't going to like having a baby. Why should he? He doesn't like his job, doesn't like who he is, is always out of sorts about money, and any threat of her not bringing in her share—however baseless such a threat might be (like her mother would refuse her maternity leave)—triggered his insecurity, his immature something. *Face it, your husband's not old enough to be a father,* she thought with a snicker.

Maybe dear Jude from long ago, Marian considered as she backed into the rush of warm water. As an only child, Jude, hey Jude, had been a make-believe friend with whom she shared confidences, sleep-overs, backseats of cars, and it tickled her to think of resurrecting Jude as one with whom to share irreverent notes on what was happening. Her mother was in no way inept as a secret sharer, she'd have to admit, and it amazed her that the woman who read her like a book had yet to figure out what was going on. Soon enough, Marian thought—and all the more reason to get her told. But Ron first, or her mother? A revealing question, wouldn't you say, she imagined inquiring of Jude, aware that her every impulse thus far had gone not to telling Ron at all but to embracing her mother in celebration and squealing like a schoolgirl. *I'm going to have a baby!*

Marian turned off the water, hung back her head and squeezed her hair. She laughed, as if Jude, close by, were holding a finger to her lips. *Yeah, it's not real funny, is it,* Marian thought. If only it were.

As she stood drying herself, the bathroom door opened. Ron entered, and she said, "Do you mind?"

"Tinkle time . . . like to scope some flesh while I'm at it."

Tell him right now, Marian said to herself. *Get it over with.* She caught him staring at her breasts and left the room. "We need separate bathrooms," she said over her shoulder.

A moment later he was at the bedroom door where, slipping on panties, she turned the other way. "Separate bathrooms, you're so spoiled," he said.

She said nothing, proceeded to fix her bra.

"Working late tonight?" he said, lingering there.

"Don't I always?"

"Can't you ever get your own mother to give you better hours?"

"Why would she do that?"

"Yeah, she'd have to pay someone some real money."

It was old banter between them but, preoccupied, Marian let her end dangle. Ron enjoyed digging at her mother, more than she liked, though Marian had been the one to identify her job as a graduation gift she had never asked for, as indentured slavery, as security for life, her life. More than once, feeling frisky over drinks, she had raised her glass and recited, "Happy graduation. That's the cash register, those are the customers, enjoy your life."

Proceeding to dress, Marian wished Ron would just go away. When he did not, when he remained about the doorway, a harder thought crossed her mind: She had no wish to tell him what was happening because she did not want him as the father of her child.

"I have to hurry," she said aside.

"Yeah yeah," he said and finally retreated downstairs.

It's true, she thought: Her one deep-seated problem with having a baby was an awareness of Ron being locked in as husband and father. Not wanting him may have been grossly unfair—he was the father—but he was also the one who personified grossness, immaturity, who appeared doomed to being unable ever to grow up. What if the baby were a girl? Marian thought. Dear God, what if it was a boy and Ron indoctrinated him to car repair, and the two of them compelled her to live in a world of rusting hulks in the yard?

At last, giving Ron a good-bye kiss on the cheek and stepping into the unusual autumn air, Marian's thoughts ran to her father, as they nearly always did on some perception of sky, breeze, or water. They were the forces with which her father lived as a lobsterman, and though she had spent but one summer working with him on the boat, their presence remained indelible. And now, of course, as if she did not have enough on her mind, she knew that her father was sick in some way and knew, too, that she needed to take some action, call or visit, or raise questions with her mother. There had been his cornhusk wheezing cough the last time she spoke to him—she called every couple weeks; he never called her—and only yesterday, entering the Weathervane for lunch, Debbie Savan, from high school, exiting, had said, "How's your dad? I saw him at the clinic."

Fine as far as she knew, Marian had thought, and a moment later, recalling his cough, began worrying, then knowing that something was wrong with her father. What clinic?

Hey Jude, help me out here, will you? she imagined saying. She had bent into the driver's seat, and in new awareness of her belly being near the steering wheel, it came to her that she had to get people told or the evidence would rise like dough and tell on itself. That and her father. And Ron. *Jude, what good are you if you can't help a person erase a few problems?*

As she backed around, yet another lingering problem touched Marian's mind: The old charge of being spoiled. She'd heard it many times, felt guilt over it often and, every time it surfaced, wanted to call time out and declare that the charge was not quite fair. So a person happened to be born other than poor, or came into the world with modest advantages, did it mean a person wasn't subject to fears and frustrations like anyone else? *Jude, tell me you understand,* she imagined adding, while Jude—not unlike any friend she had ever had—elected for the moment to be occupied with something outside her window. When you started complaining about advantages, distractions along the road always had a way of capturing your audience.

Why did so many things have to be so troublesome? Marian wondered. All on top of having a baby, and here, all at once, coming to the fore: Guilt over her father. Responsibility had her in its grip—he *was* her father—and was refusing to leave her alone. She had to talk to him on the phone, call his doctor, speak to her mother. If something were wrong, would anyone in the world be more likely than her father to deny it, even to himself?

Turning onto the highway, speeding up, then slowing down, it also occurred to Marian that her car—a ragtop Miata, the real graduation gift from her mother and Virgil—was too zippy and sporty and wasn't her anymore. Like her fear for her father's health and her wish to make up with him, everything seemed to extend from her condition. Her life was becoming an emotional, maternal bubble, threatening more each day toward popping.

Was it the baby, she wondered, catching herself straying toward the center line, or was she herself coming of age? She imagined her mother and Virgil grinning, noting that something like the latter might be the case. She could also see her mother taking it all too seriously, getting her aside and asking if she couldn't try a little harder to be more personable, more upbeat—did she see how good it was for business, how each customer was an individual friendship to be formed, how customers might come back for years, might send their children and grandchildren back forty years from now? Did she know that hardly fifty years ago old Leon Bean himself had had but a family enterprise given to high customer satisfaction? Did she see how simple it all could be? Didn't it just make her blood run to see what could be done if you put your mind to it?

Yeah, right, it made her blood run, Marian thought.

The sorry truth, she feared—following around the Kittery traffic circle—was that she wasn't cut out for commerce at all. Her mother had but vaguely minded her not studying marketing and sales in college—the acquisition of the degree itself had been key to her mother—and for her part Marian rationalized that she would grow into business while in fact, now more than ever, she'd rather sit on a dock on a lovely day like this and commune with Virginia Woolf or Annie Dillard, or a book of poems, than crow over record sales of holiday goblets. She knew it made her more like her father, for whom the quiet independence of fishing was everything; it wasn't something she'd readily say to her mother, but she knew it was true.

WARREN

Headed for the Blue Fin loading dock, he guided the *Lady Bee* at a speed hardly raising a wake. Resting against a swivel stool he had installed years ago, he kept a hand on the '68 Buick steering wheel, took in the air, and gazed within as he maintained a course he had followed into Portsmouth Harbor several thousand times, in childhood, adolescence, young manhood, maturity. His cough erupted then like a bark from an old dog, broke from his lungs and as if from the depths of the sea. It's happening, he thought. He was turning the corner.

Still the air remained calm, and he couldn't help thinking yet again how satisfying it would be to putt unto an October horizon forever. All he had ever worked for would be gone from him before long and he wondered once more if it had been his impulse to possess her that had cost him that prize of life in the first place. A country song he'd heard at the diner—she'll never be yours if you can't let her go—came to mind and he knew he was guilty to a degree. His being possessive was what she had charged while he believed, still, that her disloyalty with that eel who was her boss lay at the core of their marriage being such a failure.

Well, what does it matter now, and why keep fighting it? Nothing can likely be made right with her anyway, and what a dream it would be to sail on forever and have the old disappointments and resentments disappear in his wake.

The *Lady Bee* pulled along a dozen gulls like kites on strings. They squawked, flapped, dove like fighter planes as Warren eased a quarter turn to starboard to make a cross-tide approach to the wharf. He coughed some more. Passing a channel marker, he glanced beside the *Lady Bee*'s windshield; the hull slapped water and as usual delivered a spray of mist to his face, and the balmy air kept suggesting a peacefulness at odds with the tangled lines in his heart. Helen at the diner. Divorced with two children. She was long gone now, who knew where, but something in her smile, in her refilling of his coffee mug, had told him he'd have had a chance with her. Wasn't she the kind of woman a fisherman was meant to marry?

The hull plowed on and the breeze was countering by less than a knot. The swollen harbor yet again resembled a glassy infield tarpaulin, and back to the south, Warren thought, in Baltimore, New York, wherever it was, vendors and grounds keepers were gearing up for an afternoon game. Early fans would be loitering about a greasy

ballpark's shaded ramparts and balconies, avoiding their
seats for a while and both wanting and not wanting the
players to trickle forth and engage in infield and hitting
practice on a precious green lawn. There would be the
intoxication of youth, soil, grass, while the game—a lesson he knew too well—could only conclude and disperse
the loitering fans back to the hard streets and jobs they
had escaped, never having touched foot or finger to the
youthful turf or its sandy border and manicured infield.
Leaning out from the protection of the windshield, Warren all at once thought he detected a sound, a stadium's
roar rising over the harbor—a chill raced down his spine—
and he wondered why a sound of the kind might be visiting at a time like this. Could there be a supreme power
after all, and was he being given a sign?

Baseball had been big in Warren's life, though long
ago, and he sensed a circling back as if in a dream. The
ball field had been his boyhood preoccupation until his
father died, when he had put away his bats, cleats, first
baseman's glove, and never unbagged them again. And
though he listened to their games, he had declined giving his heart to the Red Sox in the intervening years; he
had been too serious as a player to be a fan and hadn't
been to Fenway Park more than half a dozen times in three
decades, always alone and always feeling haunted. He had
been only once with Beatrice, when they were a young
couple and the guests of her first employer, State Repre-

sentative Virgil Pound, and his wife, Abby. Warren had
hardly had a clue about illicit love or political power at
the time, and he wondered still again, barking another
cough, how things might have gone had he had but a
notion of the skulduggery of which Virgil was capable.
Being so attentive. His constant smile. The mere thought
of him, after all these years, had Warren tightening his
jaw yet again. If he could go back in time he'd pound that
politician into lobster bait, he thought. He and Beatrice
would have a life without him. Like night and day. Sailing with the breeze. Senator Pound swallowed by the
shimmering sea.

It was early to be checking out—not even ten o'clock—
and Warren's catch was meaningless. Less than a dozen,
and all small. Still, and but for his coughing, he proceeded
into the old routine without complaint. He hadn't told a
soul of the biopsy and what was happening—as if he had
anyone besides Beatrice in mind. There was Marian to tell,
though Beatrice had so attached their only child that
Warren remained uncertain even today if Senator Pound
had not cast the deciding vote there too, no matter the
crazed blood test of two decades ago.

Easing back the throttle, letting the *Lady Bee* obey
her onward motion, Warren saw, alas, that underneath it
all he was inclined toward accepting his fate because so
much of his life had been given to tasting the salt of re-

jection. Whatever you do now, go with dignity, he told himself. Don't even think of what's happened because it's history and may never be undone. Rise above resentment and go as a gentleman. Cuckold will be one perception, but some people, if you let them, will understand. What choice do you have than to hope that a handful of fellow fishermen and a few strangers will understand and validate your life?

Letting the engine bubble as he tied alongside, Warren turned off the motor and set about counting and checking the bands on his meager catch. Nine chix. His numbers were coming up short in all ways and not one of the little baseball gloves out of the deep would make a pound. Not earnings enough to cover bait and gas, though that was an old lament and he had bigger fish to fry. What did he care if he made gas money? And why that roar of the crowd at a time like this? Did his unmedicated condition have him hallucinating? A siren call urging a manly way out? Should he go down to the sea with his boat and gear and take his memories with him? Should he let some bubbles, and oblivion, be his only reply? Did he have a choice?

Hefting the crate onto the dock, Warren extended his feet and climbed out, his breath filling his own ears. Using both hands he lugged his catch into the weighing station to receive credit on the books and a chit to place with others

—money in the bank—in that certain location in his wallet. To think that modest lifting and climbing of the kind would exhaust him. If his capacity to breathe was going so quickly, how could his diagnosis come up anything but hopeless—and would the doc grant him not a measure of months or weeks, but merely of days?

There was water on the cement floor and, in the big tanks, dark lobster shapes crawled the backs of others. The room remained empty until DiMambro Jr., minding things for his father during the off-hour, came out to check and weigh his catch. "Mr. Hudon, how goes it?"

Warren couldn't help grinning at the strapping young man who had been a schoolboy ballplayer himself, famous for lacing line drives over the fence at Leary Field. "Gone better," he said.

"Well, think of the days when there's nothing at all."

"Seen my share of those," Warren said. The remarks had been repeated down through the years, while no one would address the obvious—that he was checking out early and had to have left traps unattended. Questionable work—like failing health—was something any fisherman would notice and never mention to the guilty party. Among fishermen your business was your business. Still, they all knew what was up and Warren knew they knew. You kept such things to yourself.

Loners all, Warren thought, returning to his boat. If you weren't a loner in the beginning, fishing would have its way with you in time. If your wife didn't hook up by shortwave, who but yourself would you ever have a chance to get to know?

Cranking up the old straight six, Warren untied and pushed off, motoring once more through the warm autumn air. How many times had he headed home like this—thinking of Beatrice? His life as a fisherman had been marked by smells, and in the early days when he returned home from boat, bait, and fish, there had been aromas about her he had found hard not to lick after like a dog. Perfume, cologne, hair rinses—they were as fresh as petals opening on shore and from the beginning he had loved the idea of her as his wife, had relished the smell of her. The odors of fishing were usually foul, while her smell, like her smile in those early years, had been irresistible to him, even magical. To think he had loved her as madly as any woman might wish to be loved, and that she had turned away and taken up with someone else. To think that on a hundred occasions, passing on the stairs or in the kitchen, thoughts had stolen into his mind of taking up a butcher knife and plunging it into her chest. They were the surprises of life he had never been able to sort out. Dear Beatrice. He might forgive all she had done if she would let him, but then it came to him again, a vision over the water, how helpless he was against both loving

and despising her. Would she even care that his life was
ending? Why in the world would she?

BEATRICE

Leaning for a view through her office door to see Marian
arrive, unlock the second door, and turn on lights, she
called, "Morning, honey, be out in a minute," and returned
to finishing her things-to-do list. A minor item: Yesterday
afternoon there in her office she had snapped at Virgil
for speaking unkindly (again) of Warren and was wondering if she owed him an apology, however offhanded
it might appear. Snapping was out of character for her,
certainly with Virgil, which had her thinking a word was
in order. "I did marry him," she bristled when Virgil had
remarked, "Has he ever planned anything?"

At issue was the possibility of Warren being sick—it
was nothing they had mentioned to Marian—and, if so, if
he knew the extent of his own health benefits through
the Fisherman's Co-op? "It feels *awful* to hear things like
that about him," she told Virgil, as the exchange had
opened the vein of guilt she tried always to keep closed.
"You know I bear responsibility—he didn't have to turn
out like that."

After a moment, Virgil had said, "As matter of fact
I don't think you do bear any responsibility at all. War-

ren made his choices. He's not a child." They frowned
if off, and Beatrice had begun at once to think she had
overreacted.

Yes, she'd apologize, she thought, but then, as it
happened, when the phone rang and it was Virgil calling
to set a time for lunch, he was immediately telling a joke.
"Listen, do you know the epitaph the hypochondriac had
put on his tombstone?"

"Epitaph on his tombstone—should I?"

"It's cornball, but I'm trying to brighten your day
here."

"The epitaph on the hypochondriac's tombstone?"

"*See!*"

She chortled.

"A little before one," he said. "And how about the
Galley Hatch—it's a drive but it's always pleasant."

Virgil was right, he had brightened her day. "I'm
anxious about this talk," she said.

"With your nerves of steel?"

"Don't I wish."

"The Thomaston account doesn't make you anxious?"

"What's a few hundred thousand dollars next to giving a talk to a roomful of nineteen-year-olds? It's the half-
educated girl giving-a-speech syndrome."

"You'll know five times as much as all of them put
together, believe me," Virgil said. "It's natural to feel some
stage fright. Take it from a veteran—it's positive energy

and will feed you like a drug. You'll be a hit, and we'll celebrate at lunch."

Before going on the floor—to let Marian know she'd be taking a ninety-minute lunch—Beatrice continued to feel amused and anxious as she browsed through folders for her afternoon appointments. Scandia, Parker-Smythe, the computer tutorial. Nothing pressing but she also wanted to study before the computer kid came and thought she was a dope about broadsheets and accounts payable; it seemed to be his angle on things, though it may have been her own self-consciousness. The twerp. At the same time Virgil more than broadsheets was occupying her mind. Where did he come up with that malarkey—and his self-confidence? It had impressed her in the beginning and did so still. Talking to him was like turning on a TV game show host who never missed a beat. She liked it, she'd have to admit, though she knew some people thought it was slick. Sour grapes, she thought. Life was grim enough, and as long as you got the job done what was wrong with being quick with social skills and having a good time? They were Virgil's gifts in any case, not that she'd tell him (he whom Marian and the clerks called The Virgil) for he was conceited enough as it was.

But maybe she would tell him, she thought, heading onto the floor. The things you took for granted—didn't they need to get said? For she had never really told Virgil of her appreciation for what he had done for her, the good times and success he had brought her way. She wouldn't be telling it to the young women at McInnes Business College but she wouldn't be where she was today if it hadn't been for Virgil Pound. And no matter what Warren thought, it was Virgil's friendship more than anything that she had found gratifying. Certainly she adored him, but first of all he was the best friend she had ever had. The day she walked into his office had changed her life; something came alive in her and neither of them had ever been the same. They had clicked like Fred and Ginger, as Virgil liked to say—and what was an aspiring young dancer to do, click with her dream partner and walk away?

Marian appeared unimpressed with the joke and Beatrice said, "I guess you heard it." Lori was also on the floor, as were five or six customers, strolling and browsing. Beatrice waved a greeting to Lori.

"Mom, I think I need to talk to you," Marian was saying.

"Of course, about what?"

"A couple things, this and that. Virgil, too—I'd like to talk to both of you if I can."

"Something serious?"

"I don't know—I guess so. Will Virgil be around? You're giving that talk, aren't you."

"The seminar at McInnes—I'm leaving in a few minutes. Why don't you come with us for lunch." Leaving the store with neither of them present was against Beatrice's policy but something in Marian's voice had her ignoring her own rule. "What's the subject? You'll have me worrying all morning."

"It better wait—but don't worry about it."

"You feeling down?"

"I don't know—maybe—I don't think so. Okay, I'm feeling like an elevator."

Beatrice whispered, "Honey—not that I haven't said it a few times before, but it *is* an investment, showing spunk and personality. You want to get ahead in life, in business—I keep learning this over and over. It takes effort but it's money in the bank. In the end, it's happiness."

"Mom, you know what—they should have you as a guest speaker at McInnes Business School!"

A customer with a forced smile and raised hand was signaling from the table of pepper grinders and Beatrice went to serve her, still wondering what was going on with her daughter. Ron? Her job? And wanting Virgil present?

Beatrice rang up a twenty-six-dollar sale, just as cash register one was also singing its little tune—she liked serving customers, cherished the melody of the money machines—and her thought was to explain to Marian, again, how people *gravitated to someone* who laughed, who had personality, who wasn't maybe too droll. (Unlike the way they responded to dark clouds like her father, which Beatrice but rarely pointed out.) It was the reason some succeeded and gained personal pride—they were well liked and people *enjoyed* doing them favors, sending business their way. It was satisfying to make someone smile, and the friendships that developed were real no matter what the cynics might have to say. What was wrong with getting an extra little something out of life?

MARIAN

Helping a white-haired lady select a pepper mill, and however distracted she felt, Marian couldn't resist joking. The lady was beautifully dressed all in gray, rich tweeds and satins, had stockinged canes for ankles, and of a pepper mill the size of a tenpin Marian confided: "It doesn't come with a spray but you could always hit him over the head with it." A titter came from the lady, then stifled giggling. "That's a lovely idea," she said. "That's just what I've been looking for."

In a moment, as the lady carried away a wrapped parcel in a *Maine Authentic* bag, Marian was without customers and needed—as trained by her mother—to elect a productive way to occupy herself. Lori and John, another part-time clerk who had come on, were likewise without customers at this early hour, and were dusting and straightening display shelves beyond cash register two. Down time wasn't anything Marian minded. Mornings in off-season remained a favorite time, occasions of letting her mind travel as it wished, and as she took to rearranging place mats on shelves it was more to weigh the questions in her mind, to get them to settle into neat stacks of their own.

Isolate the problem and don't kid yourself about it. It wasn't something she had learned at the University of Maine but from her mother, reinforced by who knew how many minilectures.

Her deceit in living with Ron, guessing he'd work out as a father: Was there any doubt that he was one of her core problems? And yes, it would be wise, if embarrassing, to confide the worry to her mother and Virgil. Ron had been not just slow to evolve but seemed to have stopped altogether, she thought, maybe two years earlier, when they had been married but a handful of months. The honeymoon had ended all at once for her—on his brutal smashing to the floor of a glass bowl filled with stale pasta, complaining about waste. Blinking, stepping aside in the kitchen, she had seen that she was living with an arrested adolescent. The incident evaporated but thereafter every time she looked at him she saw him differently, as if he were not as old as she had thought him to be. She tried to shed the perception, then Ron would be Ron—always seething just under the surface—and she could not help seeing that life *with* him was what was hopeless.

What to do in such a situation? Yeah, get pregnant, she told herself as she shifted back to the cash register to wait on a customer. Brilliant, given that the last thing Ron would be able to tolerate would be a child. Had she ever in her life done anything more dumb?

It was odd, too, she thought, returning to the place mats, to think how bold and mature Ron had looked to her in high school, how she had been mad for him from her two-year distance of ninth to eleventh and tenth to twelfth grades. Even when they were at Orono together and he squeezed out two years in automotive engineering before returning to Kittery to join an antique car restoration business (really to be a mechanic in charge of three hourly-rate teenage grease monkeys), she had kept believing he would break through like some famous engineer at Ford or Mercedes-Benz. It wasn't to be. He continued to live like a college sophomore—the way he lived today, sleeping in on any excuse, doing nothing at all that would get him anywhere. Seething—even when he smiled or spoke in an ordinary voice. She could *see* his suppressed anger. The only time he was not seething was when he was with his dopey friends and they were joking about cutting the cheese, burping, tailgating elderly drivers on the road.

Her father. There was her other core problem, for as much as his health was an unanswered question it was already heavy, for her, with guilt. Again, he *was* her father, and she *knew* he was sick, and also knew that if she did not assume some responsibility for him, no one would, least of all her mother. They might reside in the same house but he no more lighted up her radar than would a man living two streets away. *There's a marriage,* Marian thought. *There's an example of why you should endure, say, for the sake of the child.*

In a while, Marian thought—when her mother had left to give her talk—she would slip into the office and telephone her father at home. He could be there, if he was sick, and, whatever might be done for him, maybe she'd at least be able to sort it out and then get her mother and Virgil involved. They wouldn't like it, but no matter, her father had been treated like excess baggage, had lived the most miserable life imaginable, and the least they could do was give him some of their time. Would he be pleased that she was having a baby? Would he see a chance, in a grandchild, of his life and lineage being not entirely negative? If the child were a boy—would it make him happy if they used his name, say, as a middle name? Dear God, if she felt besieged with her problems, how might her father feel with his?

Their one abiding experience together as father and daughter—the summer she went on his boat with him as first mate—was one she had been recalling as often recently as once a day. And as she proceeded to another shelf of place mats, leaving the next customers to Lori to check out, she opened herself to the memory yet again, recalled the smell of salt water and air, the faint chill always riding the breeze and satisfaction in him being right with her as his daughter. The *Lady Bee*. She was twelve and thirteen that summer—her birthday fell on July 1st—and if anyone thought it was a picnic out on the water they didn't know her father.

Work. Learn. Remember. He made her master everything from operating boat and motor to using the fire extinguisher, throwing the O-ring to a man overboard, sending an SOS, operating ship-to-shore, responding to an SOS, abandoning ship—went into the water himself, to have her throw the ring and use a grappling hook, and had her abandon ship in a drill of her own, pulling off her rubber boots and apron and, entering the cold water in her life jacket, receive the O-ring as he tossed it twenty feet to where she was bobbing and her teeth were chattering. The exercise created a blowup at home: She's *twelve years old!* her mother had cried, while her father had growled—had bite in his growl in those days—that the idea of marine safety was to save a person's life *before* it was lost or they wouldn't stand a chance.

She had also to master the use of wrenches and tools in removing seawater from the carburetor and restarting the boat's engine . . . everything a first mate had to know and be responsible for, her father kept telling her, and, like bobbing in the water, however uncomfortable the lessons, in the aftermath they filled her with self-confidence. It was one of those fatherly things women rarely have a feel for on their own, she thought. Her mother could rail about a twelve-year-old being put into the water but in truth she overcame fears that would have left her intimidated and paralyzed. Now she'd welcome a crisis, just to show her stuff—and to make her father proud.

Nor had it been all drills, rehearsals, baiting pots. He indulged her child's need for a snooze each time out (they usually left the house at four a.m.), fixed a shelf-bunk for her on the starboard side of the *Lady Bee*'s pilothouse, out of the wind, and when she took a nap managed to wheel about so toasty sun would keep her warm within the enclosure and make her snoozing easy. And he called her "sleepytime girl" when she stirred to her feet; gave her sips of coffee from his big thermos (leading to another spat at home), loved her unequivocally in those waking-up moments, though calling her "sleepytime girl" was as close as he ever came to getting it into words.

Life had betrayed her father. Given half a chance he might have been twice the man he came to be. Fate was cruel. Who would believe he had lived all his life in a house with a wife who had given herself, body and soul, to another man? It wasn't how it happened on television. On television a man might rage in the face of such obstacles. Around the harbor, and but for his damaged spirit,

her father went about his business. He was a defeated man.
It was both painful and true.

Customers began to multiply and Marian returned to serving them while her thoughts roamed. Who would she be
today, she wondered, had she gone into fishing with her
father? Who would her father be—he who had not had a
son to take into his business? Would he be a happy and
vigorous man? Something independent and wild about
lobstering appealed to Marian, especially there in the careful store with its scented cosmetics and candles—called
to her more strongly than marketing, than being dressed
and delicate, serving people with smiles rather than jokes,
those parts of the business she had never quite liked. If
there was a boy in her, she thought, maybe it was telling
her to be reckless and strong, to head into life directly
and openly. As a mother on her way to childbirth, she
felt certain of one thing: If she had a boy or a girl, the call
of the sea this summery day had an adventurous feel for
her, while work in the aromatic store felt layers removed
from what was rich and vital.

Stealing office time, leaving Lori and John to cover floor
and cash registers, Marian telephoned her parents' home,
and replaced the receiver when the answering machine
clicked on. Then she telephoned her father's doctor, told
the receptionist she was Warren Hudon's daughter, and

asked if they knew what was going on with her father, if he had been referred to a clinic?

"The Kittery Clinic, I believe," a woman named Pricilla told her.

"The cancer clinic?" Marian's worst fear felt confirmed.

"It sounds like he hasn't told you very much."

"He's very secretive."

"Well, gee, listen, I'll give you their number, but I don't think they'll tell you anything over the phone."

And so it was. Identifying herself yet again as Warren Hudon's daughter, she asked for an update on her father's condition, and the receptionist said, "I'm sorry, we can't give out information like that over the phone."

"I *am* his daughter," Marian said.

"Well, his chart says no family," the woman said, as if reading from a screen.

Marian sighed. "No family? Is it blank or does it say that?"

"No family is checked."

"Does it mean he said that?"

"That I couldn't tell you."

"Could I speak to the oncologist?"

"Dr. Dawson's with a patient right now."

"Does it mean my father has cancer?"

"Miss, you need to ask your father to have your name added to his file, so you can have access to information about his condition. I'd be glad—Dr. Dawson's assistant would be glad—to share information with you, but it does say no family on the screen."

"But he has cancer—isn't that the only reason he'd be there?"

"Miss, listen, I understand your frustration, but you'll need to speak to your father, or to Dr. Dawson. I have other calls here. Patients do come in for consultations—it doesn't mean they're diagnosed with cancer."

"You can't just tell me?"

"Miss, please. You'll have to speak to Dr. Dawson."

Running through Marian's mind as she returned to the checkout counter was a thought of Virgil having influence enough to make a call and have people vie with information. Then she thought no, saw that using Virgil to learn something about her father wasn't the way she wanted to go.

WARREN

In Narrow Cove, returning in the direction of open water, he tied to his float and let the *Lady Bee* swing to anchor. Then he did something uncharacteristic—he sat on the gunwale to rest and contemplate the path his life had taken. Securing the boat had exhausted his breath yet again, though for the moment his confusion was lifting away. Placid water in the cove was soothing at high tide, given the warmth of the air. Try to be as calm as the weather, he thought—for what was more worth savoring at this late stage than an Indian summer reprieve? His doctor's appointment wasn't until one-fifteen and he had nothing to do in the meantime but take in breaths of air, as if to store for later use, and to keep the runaway freight-train coughing from taking him on breathless rides. Taking him, he sensed, into swirls where one day soon he would experience darkness from which there would be no return.

Warren hated to admit it, but he knew his anxiety was tied still to the disgusting folly he had committed, the self-loathing he had imposed on himself, in letting Virgil Pound arrange a job for him twelve years ago with the state. Eight years in the Water Pollution Division. He had sold out—there was no getting around it. Maybe he broke away in time but he had yet to regain his bearings. Wearing the uniform, that cap of a cuckold. A job arranged by Senator Pound. An employee protected by Senator Pound— so the senator might have his way with the employee's sexy little wife. Would selling out ever settle itself in his mind?

Virgil may have come to him and he may have acted forthright and independent but they both knew who was pulling the strings. Everyone knew, just as they knew his wife worked for the influential politician and traveled as his assistant, his companion and mistress. His whore. Why *not* take the job? Warren told himself at the time. Lobster

catches were down, he was scraping by and being made
a fool of—why not gain some financial security in the
terrible mix of things? What was the alternative—to leave
Beatrice and take up solitary life in a saltwater shed, become another mad dog Mainer made simple by the muck
and brine left exposed at low tide?

All along there had been the richness of the dark sea
calling to him with its mystery and depth. The sea had
filled his life, and at times he had hated it, but then it
had never presented more meaning to him than when
he was away from it, or on glorious days like today.
Cough-free for the moment—the train in his throat seeming to glide over a prairie—he gazed beyond the watery
darkness to where the tide had left ribbons on sea walls,
and on the spit of land where his truck was parked a
hundred yards distant and a fathom higher. Creatures of
all kinds luxuriated within the deep, and the sea's tidal
movement had been growing no less than spiritual to
him in its immensity. The body of water was like an
organism too vast to comprehend.

He watched it rise, like the side of a cat—a watery
kingdom from which life had come gasping and crawling
millions of years ago. He liked the idea of tides being earth
breathing, and returning there himself to disappear. But
he also wanted to remain with Beatrice, to lie in proxim-
ity to her, thinking they might yet reconcile, along the path

to eternity. Or to be lying next to her when the sea came in to claim them both. Never having possessed her in life—in body early on, but never in spirit—he felt all the more bewildered at the thought of being apart from her in death each time it came to mind. Being cheated was the story of his life and here, turning into the home stretch, he was finding himself haunted with issues of mortality he had barely considered since childhood. He did not quite believe in hell, or in purgatory, rather he saw oblivion, aloneness and loneliness, as the alternative to a heaven offering some form of consciousness. How could the universe ever stop unfolding—and who could know what waited in the infinite beyond? Who could know that those who had been cheated in life might not gain some justice in the hereafter?

It would be fine to have the lights fade without warning, Warren thought, though there was something to be said for knowing ahead of time and having a chance to make peace with yourself—as he was striving to do. He'd never be able, in this life or the next, to accept what she and Virgil had done to him—their stunting of his heart—but it wasn't them alone that concerned him now. He kept trying to bring a larger picture into focus. Hearing the roar of the crowd, wondering if a phantom audience had at long last decided to tally the score of his life. His thoughts and fears about dying had him feeling human for the first time in years, sensing freedom of a kind he had forgotten existed.

Time to have strong drinks and hear strong music, he thought. Time to shed bittersweet tears and let his heart open all the way. *Dear God, please release me,* he cried to himself, looking down his front. *Please release my locked-up heart and let it live again.*

Fifty-seven was young by today's measure, but not so brief in the time mortals had on earth. It was hard to believe his father had lived to but fifty-two, though he had seemed old to Warren when he came down sick— leukemia had been the diagnosis—and died but days later. Half a century still seemed a lifetime on earth, no matter how you cut it. Compressed today, maybe, but a full turn nonetheless. If you hadn't done what you wanted by fifty, chances were you had spent your chances. Think of the Indians, who would have been relics at fifty, Warren thought, or of the current life expectancy of seventy-six or so, and half a century still looked like a reasonable run.

Getting the obituary blues, he thought. He grinned to himself and thought of telling the line to Beatrice— after all, she was his wife—letting her know that the end didn't have to be so solemn. The thought seemed to nudge him onto another train spur of barking and disrupted his intoxicating sentiment, the best time it seemed he'd had

in a month of Sundays. Getting acquainted with mortality. Morose pleasure. What phase was this?

Warren finished tying down the *Lady Bee*'s pilothouse and,
swallowing a shallow breath, pushed the dinghy into the
water. His thoughts were on times in the past when things
had been wonderful between them. More than just respect,
she had loved him once, he was certain. It had to do with
this very boat, which had defined who he was even in
high school, when they had first gotten together. His father had been dead a year and he was the only boy in
high school running a full-time business on the side—
early-morning and late-evening hours—though he ran no
traps at all from December into March when he under-
took boat maintenance and trap repair for the coming
season. Beatrice had been impressed, as had others. His
industriousness led to the Phelps Award at graduation,
when the principal said to the full gathering that Warren
Hudon was a credit to the school and the community. He
was six-two and skinny at the time, and the long hours
had come easily to him, not excluding playing first base
on the school team in the spring and in Legion ball during the summer. That senior year would turn out to be
the high point of his life did not come home to him until
he was in his forties.

   There had been another moment, one dawn as he
left the house, when his mother told him from the heart

he was the best son a mother could ever wish to have. And another moment when Beatrice took him home to meet her parents, and exclaimed, "Warren's the only boy in school who already has his own business!" But his best moment was when it came to him, age nineteen, to name his boat and business for his teenage bride-to-be. The *Lady Bee*. His eyes had filmed over then and grew misty here again, as he dragged the dinghy to his truck and hefted it in. The *Lady Bee*. Had anything ever been more satisfying than that moment of inspiration?

Upon a week of painstaking stencil-taping along the bow and across the stern there came the painting and drying of the letters, the buffing with wax to protect the paint from the elements. Then came the time to drive Beatrice to Narrow Cove for the presentation, when the boat's angle would be just right as she uncovered her eyes, as she stared, caught her breath, and appeared more thrilled than he had been himself. The only schoolboy to have his own business had stood there with existence in his hand, in 1958.

They married that summer and Beatrice began her two-year college business program in the fall, while he added gangs of gear, joined the Fisherman's Co-op, and worked long hours to live up to expectations. Earning her associate's degree, she answered an ad for a job in the offices of Virgil Pound who, not yet thirty, was already the father of three, a practicing attorney and, from the

Thirty-sixth District, a recently elected state representative to the Maine State Legislature.

Who could have guessed what lay before them—tossed by the sea, harrowed by winds of lying, deception, rejection? What a fine young couple they made, everyone liked to say. What a future they had before them. Who would have guessed it would come to this? How could a politician like that just have his way with another man's wife? Why had she gone over to him as she had? Who knew the answers to such impossible questions?

BEATRICE

The young women seemed to like her well enough but not as much, at first, as she had been prepared to like them. She believed she was lively, warm, coherent and, as Virgil had said, that her stage fright gave her a charge that worked to her advantage: an independent businesswoman letting them know they could make it on their own in a man's world—if they were willing to give it their all! Most of them appeared more vague, however, than captivated.

Were they distracted? Slightly vacant? Had she grown more educated and removed from them than she had realized? After all, nine years had slipped by since her own daughter had been their age in college. Too bad she couldn't describe the Thomaston account—the wooden

candle holders, lamps, salt and pepper shakers to be produced in red oak and maple laminations by inmates at
the Maine State Prison—but Maine Authentic's move for
an exclusive agreement was still up for approval and not
to be disclosed.

"A Business of One's Own" was the banner under
which she made her presentation—a thirty-minute talk to
be followed by thirty minutes of coffee klatching—and
there was smiling and laughter but only two or three of
the twenty-odd seemed to have any fire in their eyes. Were
the others half-asleep at ten a.m.? Who were they kidding
if they were dozing in business school at ten in the morning? Were they spoiled? Beatrice wasn't ready for that either, and when she finished talking and it was time for
coffee, her thought was to glide through the chatter, be
on her way, and chalk it up to differences between the
can-do and why-me generations, as Virgil liked to call
them.

There came a question from a young woman in a
slouch and all at once Beatrice decided to respond as she
would to Marian when she had been in high school. "How
do you get some senior banker to agree to a start-up loan?"
the young woman said, and Beatrice wasn't sure if the
girl was one who had paid attention or not.

"Listen to me now, because I'm going to be a little
hard on you," she said, and saw some eyes turn her way.
"You have to *look* the part—you hear what I'm saying?

You have to act, eat, drive and walk the part. It has to be in your hair—in your pantyhose, young lady, when you walk into a bank and climb a flight of stairs. If you're content to be a clerk for the rest of your life, just tune me out right now. Fresh clothes. *Nice* clothes. A sparkling car helps—something with a good name—a *Buick,* an *Oldsmobile,* a *Chrysler.* A manager's car, not a clerk's car. Appearances are especially important for women—let's face it. And to look the part you have to *be* the part *within.* That's the secret—be clearheaded and confident. Be smart. Present yourself in that way, have your act together, your homework done—be ready—and that bank manager will respect you and will be thrilled to sign. 'Yes ma'am, will that be enough?' he'll say and he'll be wishing his own daughter was half as together."

Sounds of response came from the room and, on a glance, Beatrice knew she had gained their attention; added questions came about credit, clothes, money for cars.

"Self-esteem is what every woman is aware of when she selects her outfit for the day," Beatrice said then. "You have to plan ahead and be prepared. Heaven help you if your blouse has coffee stains and you put off washing your hair because it's Friday and you're getting off early. That's laziness—go back to the end of the line. Dressing for success is step number one. Preparing the inner self. Standing tall—taller than you're standing right now—yes, you, young lady, who asked about bank loans. Being liked on the outside because you're liking yourself within. And don't tell me you can't come up with nice clothes or borrow your father's car. Do what has to be done. No excuses. Or be happy as a clerk, with stringy hair and minimum wage."

There was gasping and laughing, more questions about clothes and looking the part within, and Beatrice said, "In fact I was wrong when I said dressing for success is step number one. What is really step number one is *eating* for success, because the trimmer you are the better you'll look—and in less expensive clothes. Okay, now maybe that's sexist to have to worry about dressing and eating, I would agree—but don't we ourselves feel respect for women who have it together? I know I do— along with some envy. It keeps me going. In the battle of the bulge, don't rationalize, is what I say! Be vigilant! Savor sweat!"

Their faces were laughing, blossoming, asking about mentoring, interviewing, what employers looked for in applicants. "Okay, this is important too," Beatrice said, "and it's not *unrelated* to dressing and eating! Number one: Attitude. Spell it out to yourselves because it's everything. It means loving what you do. You can tell when someone is winging it, going through the motions. Teachers, lawyers. Clerks in stores. You can tell. Lost threads. Missed connections. Put that beside someone who is *involved* in their work and a child can tell you the difference. The young woman who is prepared and loves what she does has confidence, has style—which derives from attitude—and it doesn't matter if she's winning a case in court or selling a one-piece bathing suit. She brings *magnetism* to her life and to her employer—she'll get job offers and she'll love getting up in the morning because she knows she's good at what she does. Think about it. *Attitude.* If yours isn't one of *wanting* to do it then you're wasting your time and everyone else's. And the battle of the bulge will only be harder to win," Beatrice added, to more laughter and spontaneous applause.

When one of the young voices gushed, "Will you be my mom?" she laughed and joy filled her breast. "I'd love to if I had time," she said, and the mom exchange made her eyes gloss up as she returned across the parking lot to the shiny red LeBaron. Affection for the girls had taken her by surprise and she anticipated recounting the experience to Marian and Virgil. And she thought again that she could write a book about it. Self-taught, self-starting. Not to brag, but that would be the ticket.

VIRGIL

At the intersection leading into the Mall segment containing Maine Authentic an old Transam blasted its horn as it roared past on the shoulder, cutting off his right-of-way.

The scuzzy wreck with Maine plates was driven by a twenty-something and Virgil thought, have it your way, fella, and, in the wake of the careening car, guided his Mercedes into the parking lot with the cool, slow demeanor of a top gun riding into town.

Virgil was pleased that his big vehicle might trigger hostility. The charcoal gray S420 was a muscle car and though it wasn't what he'd drive if he were still in office, he liked that it conveyed a message. His other considerations had been a black Seville STS or a black Lincoln Continental. Nothing else was horse enough to do the job though selecting image in a car wasn't something he would readily admit. A man's car did some talking, especially in today's in-your-face world, while understatement also needed to play a part. Quiet power. People took notice when it pulled alongside. Or they spat gravel on the run like that loser in the Transam. Black leather and walnut trim. A Stealth cockpit. Dozens of instruments. A car with which to have an affair of the kind he was having. Low 70s. Paid in cash on a shifting of funds between accounts when he wrote the check and, okay, $12,000 more than he'd disclosed to either Abby or Beatrice, but worth every penny. He adored his car the way a teenager might adore an elegant woman beyond his reach, and guessed that settling into the black leather passenger seat, for a woman, was a tingling sexual experience. It sure was for him, though it was another awareness he wouldn't readily admit. When it came to power, Virgil Pound reserved an eye for details of the kind many voters felt but never took time to notice.

At least he had this, Virgil thought as he circled the lot before the store, looking for an opening and not unaware of his position and prominence. People's eyes still paused when noticing him, and remarks were uttered aside to companions. He'd never made it to the national game—his life's core regret—but it had to be acknowledged that competition at that level was ferocious and that he'd done okay in what he'd gone for. He was happy. *You're happy, aren't you?* he joked to himself as he found a space facing the store.

Pausing, spotting two former constituents he had no wish to hear out—listening politely in parking lots was one of the singular downsides to life as a public figure—Virgil acted out concern with his attaché case on the passenger seat. Shifting an eye, seeing that the coast still wasn't clear, he continued with the attaché case. Within—in no rush and in a good-humored mood this pleasantly warm day—he sensed an old interest visiting his mind: the enjoyment he experienced in exercising authority. No doubt about it, power had been a lifelong vice, and it certainly was a vice. Witness his fantasies in controlling, zapping, if he wished, Beatrice's clod of a husband and the pleasure he could derive in merely thinking what he could do to make the man's life miserable. Dim-witted Warren learning that his commercial license had expired, his bait was in violation, his traps were too large—and having no idea he was being finessed into begging to be taken back on by the Water Pollution Commission. Fantasies of the kind were one of Virgil's dirty little secrets—and, no doubt, a source of enhanced potency. The women's groups had it right in their yammering about power being an aphrodisiac—administering power was certainly one for him! However privately, he *knew* that manipulating Beatrice's husband added . . . well, ask any old pol if administering power wasn't part of the game? Of course they'd deny it— why else call it a game?

Marian's was the first familiar face Virgil saw on entering, and she said at once, "Hope you don't mind—I'm going to lunch with you and Mom. I sort of invited myself."

Virgil smiled, said, "Nothing could please me more. Gorgeous day today—beautiful."

"I won't be buying," Marian added.

Virgil chortled.

"I have some things to ask the grown-ups," Marian said and Virgil kept grinning, trying to figure out what was happening.

Beatrice appeared and he turned aside to give her a peck on the cheek. "You don't mind Marian coming along?" she whispered, and he said, "Not at all," which meant, they both knew, that he was less than thrilled. Things to ask the grown-ups? "I don't know what's on her mind," Beatrice said. "It must be Ron."

Minutes later, jackets and purses in hand, they were in the LeBaron with Beatrice behind the wheel and Virgil in back—where he did not like, ever, to be. Marian, next to her mother in front, glanced his way and smiled, looking amused at the scrunched-in sight of him. Beatrice had a quirk about driving her own car during business hours and Virgil understood, though on this outing, serving as aide to the two women, he was sorry he hadn't insisted on the security of his big gray import.

"Can we get into this now or do we have to wait?" he said.

"Honey?" Beatrice asked across the front seat.

"Can we wait?" Marian said, and added, looking to the rear, "Virgil, I'm sorry to draw you into this—I can see you just wanted to have a nice lunch, and I'm screwing it up. I'm not even sure I know what I want to say. Some headaches I'm sure you'd just as soon do without."

Virgil gave no reply, to let her know she was right— he had only wanted to have a nice lunch. Beatrice pressed south on Route 1, and looking the two women over, Virgil thought yes, it has to do with money, or with her husband. Probably both. Further, as in any state house invitation to lunch, he knew his presence was in no way casual. She's probably disillusioned with her little hubby and wants him to make it go away. Or it may be the store; she may want to leave—she's never appreciated what her mother has done for her—and go to graduate school. Probably to study philosophy, or sociology, or French literature and to say that when she has another degree she'll be ready to come back on full time and really give herself to sales. At the least the husband, Virgil thought. The marriage was faltering, he'd gotten the drift of that, and knew, too, that Beatrice had conveyed to Marian his disappointment in her choice of a mate. Maybe Marian wanted him to know he had been right in the first place, and wanted to return to his good graces. Who could blame her?

"Don't worry about lunch," Virgil said. "If we're not here for you, who is? Only next time can we go in a more comfortable car?"

Marian tittered, pleasing him. Beatrice continued driving and Virgil let his eyes once more take in the women before him, seeing again how he was being cast in the role of father. Not that he minded, because he enjoyed the cards he could play with money and authority without having to assume deep responsibility. Dopey Warren, he thought. He wouldn't have known what to do even if he'd been ashore and involved all these years, and Virgil pitied the pathetic man—so he told himself. Yet how could Warren have so failed to see, years ago, the prize he'd chanced to win for a wife? Virgil knew he'd given Beatrice more backing than most people could

afford, but at least he'd had sense enough to let her guide
her own course—like a parent stepping back from a child
risking limb, exhilaration, spunk on a two-wheeler—and
not insist on keeping his hand on her rear fender. What
gifted woman wouldn't seek to pull away? What reasonable man wouldn't let her do so? That wasn't a dirty little
secret at all, it was common sense.

"Dad's sick, did you know that?" Marian said as her mother
entered the parking lot, and Virgil thought, oh, God, that's
what it is, of course. Warren's sick—they'd known it and,
of course, hadn't known it. Virgil was only sorry—uncomfortable yet in the backseat—that he hadn't arranged
Warren's movement out of town a long time ago and had
him out of their lives.

"You mean really sick?" Beatrice was saying. "I just
saw him, two or three days ago."

"Oh, he's sick—I don't know how bad. I only know
that it's cancer, and of course he hasn't told anyone. He has
that cough—he's been coughing for weeks. But you know
how he is—I'm not surprised no one knows anything."

"You've seen him?" Beatrice said. "When I saw him
he looked like himself—though he has been coughing,
I've heard him coughing."

"Debbie Savan saw him at the cancer clinic—where
I called, but they won't tell me anything. They said, in his
file, it says no family."

"Sounds like Warren," Virgil said. "Can't get you one way he'll try another."

"Virgil, please," Marian said. "What do you expect him to do? He is my father, you know."

"Sorry, of course. Sorry—which isn't to say he hasn't always been like that." It had to be the first time Marian had ever dared speak back to him and Virgil thought, well, she has a point. "This may not be my affair," he added.

"Yes it is, Virgil," Marian said. "Listen, I'm sorry if I sound hysterical. Of course it's your affair. When he says no family, he means all of us. You know what his life has been like."

"He wants us to leave him alone?" Beatrice said.

"I'm sure he does," Marian said. "But the point is, he is sick, and we have to do something—don't you think? He needs help."

"Marian's right," Virgil said. "Of course she is. If he's sick—and I think first of all we should find out how sick he is. Before we fly off the handle. If he's sick, he certainly doesn't have anyone to turn to. No family. It's pathetic, but yes, we should do something."

Virgil feared he had offended Marian yet again, though for the moment no one said anything. Then Beatrice said, "I guess I was afraid of this. It had to happen sometime."

Once more they sat in silence, until Virgil said, "Still, you don't know what his diagnosis is? There are many kinds of cancer, you know, and some are quite treatable."

"He has that cough, I'm sure it's lung cancer," Marian said.

"Not with certainty though?" her mother said.

"Not positively, no."

"Well, we're here for lunch," Virgil said. "Or would you rather forget lunch?" He knew they wouldn't and there followed the exiting of the car. "That's what you had to tell us—your father's going to the cancer clinic?" he added as they crossed the parking lot.

"Something else, which is only partly grim," Marian said. "Virgil, I wanted to see if you could loan me a hundred thousand dollars. Just kidding, just kidding," she added.

Again she had gotten him to laugh, and he said, "Pocket change, my dear. Mere pocket change."

"Oh, I'm afraid it's the pregnancy thing," Marian announced as they settled into a booth and were in receipt of large menus. "That's the okay part, I guess."

It was a message of delayed joy and Virgil served as silent witness as Beatrice progressed from surprise to accommodation, to embracing the prospect with happy expectation and teary eyes. "Honey, that's good news," she said several times over, and Virgil got in, "Having a baby, it's one of life's basic experiences—you'll make a fine mother, Marian. Congratulations."

"A baby!" Beatrice said. "I *love* babies—a grandchild of my very own!"

Well, he had the pregnancy part right, Virgil thought, as he sat waiting for still another shoe to fall.

"We'll make everything work out at the store," Beatrice was saying. "You can take time off, do flexible hours, anything you like. We'll make it work like a dream—anything to have a little baby around!"

"Okay, what's the part that isn't okay?" Virgil said. "Let's get it over with."

There was a pause. Then Marian said, "Oh, it's Ron, and Dad being sick, too."

"Ron doesn't want the baby?" Beatrice said.

"As if I tell him anything," Marian said.

"You haven't told him?"

"Not yet. You know how immature he is. I'm just not sure about him anymore as a husband. That's the bad part. And this news about Dad. It throws everything out of sync for having a baby. I'm sorry to unload all this on you—but I thought maybe you could help."

"Honey, there're always things to deal with, if you're having a baby or not," Beatrice said. "Ron hasn't actually said anything—"

Virgil decided it was time to weigh in. "Listen . . . let's find out how sick your father is," he said. "That'll give us an idea what to do. As for Ron, Marian, you know people make mistakes in marriage all the time. If that's what has happened, you don't have to feel unique, or like you're stuck with it forever. It isn't like that anymore. He may feel the same way—you don't really know. The thing for you to understand is that your mother and I support you and will do whatever needs to be done to help you along. Okay? You worry about that baby and we'll deal with these other things as we learn more and time goes on. I mean it," Virgil added.

Marian's eyes brimmed, and she checked herself for the moment from trying to speak.

"We're on your side," Virgil said. "The store's on your side. Don't underestimate that store. And I always have my finger in a few pots. Call me any time, night or day, and I'll do whatever has to be done—just so I don't have to ride in the backseat of small cars! And please cheer up—expectant mothers are supposed to be happy."

Virgil had them smiling (liked, in himself, that he possessed authority that could turn things around) and as he squeezed Marian's hand Beatrice added her own and both women blinked against misting eyes. He could as well have just sealed key legislation, Virgil thought. "You have your life before you," he added to Marian. "I love you, you know, like my own daughter, and you're too young to be unhappy." They sustained their hand squeeze and Virgil checked his own eyes against filming over. "Can we get to these menus?" he said. "I'm starving."

WARREN

Once when he felt unable to bear it any longer he shouted at her, "My God, why don't you leave me? You have your store, your life, you have money—a lot more than I do. Why don't you go off on your own and file for divorce? Why are you doing this to me?"

She declined to respond. It had been a low-tide morning and he was late leaving the house. She regarded his outburst with a smirk, stepped past him on her way upstairs, and he felt caught, as always, in the core of his life's frustration. Wanting to smash it apart, he cried after her, "Tell me what you want from me! I have a right to know!"

If she had a reply it was not forthcoming, and moments later, returning downstairs, she left the house and drove away. They seldom spoke, and fought but rarely, and it was the first time he had called on her to leave him. Her doing so would have destroyed him, he was sure, and was what he feared in his heart he wanted her to do. His notion of Helen at the diner was merely a notion. He'd never be any good with another woman, was certain he would fail if he ever tried. Why Beatrice chose not to leave remained a mystery to him, and one he had no interest in solving.

Warren lost balance and fell to the bedroom floor while putting on his pants. He had showered and was dressing for the doctor's appointment when a foot caught—his fall due as much to lightheadedness as to the coupling of pant cuff and toe. He knocked an elbow and twisted knee and ankle going down, and, unless it was in childhood, could not remember the last time he had fallen, not even on his boat when it was smacking high seas and he had to long-step from pilothouse to gunwale and back again. The fall, within his coughing and advancing disorientation, marked his first loss of physical confidence.

Warren knew what the doctor's prognosis would be and kept trying to avoid thinking about it. Each cough seemed to leave less space in his lungs, and his body's response was the dizziness that assisted his fall. His internal system sought pockets of air when he coughed, while he had no wish to be noticed, or pitied, by anyone, least of all by Beatrice. Late evenings recently, when she was home, he had been closing himself into his bedroom and turning up the TV there, not to be heard coughing, wheezing, gasping. *She'll be happy to be done with me,* he thought, though he was growing increasingly terrified of dying without settling things between them.

He could have called the doctor or gone to the emergency room months ago, but had put it off. He had *known* there was nothing to be done. His lungs had known. His fear all along was of medical people tortur-ing him with chemicals, radiation, tubes, scrambling his

mind with drugs and confining him to bed; claustropho-
bic confinement of that kind felt more threatening than
death. He wanted his mind to travel where it would for
as long as it might, to visit that which had been meaning-
ful to him. Mindlessness fed by chemicals would not be
worth any extra days or weeks. He'd trade half an hour
thinking of his boyhood on the water, he thought, for a
month of double vision in an overheated room.

Then, driving to the clinic—his second visit that
week—the likelihood of death suddenly swept through
him as he gazed through the windshield. That she and
Virgil might live on, might joke and laugh, walk together
and eat out, might undress and embrace in bed in his own
house, made simple breathing difficult to manage. To be
a loser unto death confounded his thinking with lapses,
small explosions, crazed emotions. He had to make peace
with her. He had to.

In an examination room, stripped to the waist, Warren
wondered how Dr. Dawson would say what he had to
say. *"I'm sorry I have to tell you this."* Or, because he had
suggested that he bring his wife or closest relative for the
reading of biopsy and CAT scan: *"I really wish you weren't
hearing this alone."*

To Warren it would be just as well if the doctor came
right out and said he was doomed, and he was surprised
when the white-bearded man, slipping into the room with

laptop computer in hand, came close. Sitting in a school-type chair, lifting the computer's lid, he said, "It's oat cell—which I'm afraid is not very good news."

For a moment Warren returned the doctor's gaze, before saying, "There's no hope?"

The doctor's eyes held Warren's for an instant before he began telling of both lungs being afflicted and describing symptoms of double pneumonia. "The chest X rays show metastatic tumors in both lungs," he said on another direct gaze.

"They're malignant?"

"Multiple sites, I'm sorry to say. And it's small cell in an advanced stage. It's fast—"

"Well, it's not a surprise," Warren said.

"With chemotherapy and radiation—"

Warren raised a hand. "No need to waste your breath." He proceeded at once to his feet, started buttoning up. "Treatment's worse than the cancer, from what I've heard," he said.

"Oat cell *is* fast—"

"Gets real bad I'll give a call," Warren said. "How much time? That's what I need to know. I need to put some things in order."

The doctor was also getting to his feet, looking perturbed that his patient was walking out before he'd hardly gotten started.

"Weeks or months?" Warren said.

"Without treatment, it's—"

"Just tell me the truth."

"Without treatment—it progresses quickly," the doctor said.

"Weeks?"

"Oat cell is—"

"Days?"

"Mr. Hudon, it depends on the treatment, and on your response to the treatment. There—"

"I get the message," Warren said.

"There *are* experimental drugs—" the doctor said, but Warren was at the door. Then, in a different voice, the doctor said after him, "Mr. Hudon, listen—you have to come to terms with your life. That's what you have to do. I'm sorry."

Warren paused enough to look back.

"You asked me to speak candidly," the doctor said. When Warren did not respond, he added, "Make peace with yourself, Mr. Hudon. That's the best advice I can give you. Turn to your loved ones. And I know you have a daughter because she called earlier today. Don't try to do this on your own."

In the lobby, as Warren walked through, the receptionist called after him, "Mr. Hudon—you need to make an appointment!"

"Won't be coming back," Warren said and continued into the balmy air, carrying his death sentence like nothing else than a new jacket all at once acquired as a gift. He knew absolutely now, and as he bypassed the reflecting windows of parked cars, deep fulfillment he had not expected was flowing into him.

His daughter was a loved one, but she, too, was at a distance and he wanted to go it alone. Being alone all these years had been the true cancer of his life, though now, if only for a moment, he might gain his wife's attention—the one moment for which he had yet to live.

Warren found himself doing what he had not done in months: pausing near her store to see if Virgil's fat Mercedes was parked outside. Spotting Virgil's various cars had never been easy, for parking was always crowded at the mall leg that contained Maine Authentic. Nor would he mention it to her later if he spotted the killer whale parked nearby. This time, strangely, he *wanted* it to be there. Nor was he out to catch her, he realized, so much as to gain the psychological leverage Virgil's presence might provide—a trump card in his psyche with which to counter her authority when the time came.

He idled at the farthest distance, imagined them in her busy store joking with all those part-time clerks and customers, coming and going from her office in the rear, sitting at the coffee table there and sipping from small glasses. And all at once it came to Warren that before long he would not see Beatrice again. It came to him, as if she were a young girl again wanting only to do well in her life, that he loved her and wanted not to blame her, rather to make peace with her and forgive her. He saw himself as a dog that loved its mistress in spite of being closed into a cellar, a creature helpless against feeling gratitude when she appeared at last and offered a cup of water.

Forgiving her for his demise was not new to him, but there it was, filling his throat. He would forgive Virgil, too, alas, believing his soul was letting him know, in extremis, that in forgiveness eternal peace might be gained. The race was ending; his desire was to say good-bye and to wish them well. To die with peace in his heart.

Virgil and Beatrice. They had decades to live, and however strange their presence within him, Warren saw as if in a vision that he loved them both. His resentment was lifting like a cloud, and he loved them above all else. He might gain her respect, her friendship at last. And if there was a hereafter the two of them might reconcile in time and be together again. Life never unfolded as predicted. Who could say what lay ahead?

Dear Beatrice. His love for her, from boyhood, from young manhood down through the years, no matter her betrayal, had him gripping his face there in his pickup, wheezing above the truck's steering wheel. If he could speak to her, he thought, if he could get her to listen, he'd admit at last that in the beginning he *had* assumed ownership of her—it was true—and doing so had been wrong, especially for a young woman so bright and ambitious. He was sorry for that—if it was what had gotten between them. She and Virgil should have been together from the beginning, for they were a pair to draw to—he'd admit that too.

Maybe he'd come right out and ask that *she* forgive *him,* that she shake hands and let them both correct their sails on the way into whatever lay ahead. Might she not end up at his side—if nature took its course? Virgil, of course, would end up with Abby, and in time no one strolling past their chiseled names would know a thing. Warren, husband/Beatrice, wife. A married couple together again, sailing through timeless time side by side. Otherwise it was Warren's wish to be cast out to sea, though he knew no way of saying so without spoiling any last chance with her. Let nature take its course. On a word alone, he thought, she might quell the defeat with which, all these years, he had lived like a dog tied to a leash. He had lost the game of life and would let her go now, would forgive her and wish her well, if only, on a single word, she might allow hope and peace to enter his rattled heart. Of one thing he was certain: He would never harm her, would travel the high road every step of the way.

Intoxicated with life and death, Warren drove to Narrow Cove for the second time in one day. Sentence delivered, sentence received. Intimations of mortality were all about and he kept taking them in, gave pause over the bridge and along the waterway like any other terminal geezer giving a read to the scarcity and simplicity of existence. Life had not treated him perfectly, he thought, still he and Beatrice had met, had loved each other, married and had a child. Nor had love died, not for him. Wasn't that a credit to take into the unknown? Even the time he succumbed to whiskey and went, aroused, to her bedroom—wasn't it but an expression of his passion for her? Dear God, he had merely wanted to have his arms around her in her silken nightgown, to join with her, to transport her, to transport them both. The fool he made of himself, shoved into the hall wailing and trying flat out to embrace the surface of her door, staggering off and ejaculating like a crazed animal in his own room, knowing it was that or smashing down her door and forcing her to submit, raping her, perhaps doing more than raping her. Wasn't it merely passion, the desire any man might know for the woman he had married and adored?

Now the old Jonesporter he had named after her. The boat would need a new motor soon and, if she were going to last a couple more seasons, a new painting overall, top and bottom. She also had to be cleared out in anticipation of Beatrice putting her up for sale, and pleased to be back in the balmy air, Warren began the process of va-

cating the small and infinite world wherein he had spent
so much of his life. If he could get his life settled, he
thought he'd simply lie in peace and watch the baseball
play-offs down through the end of the season. A number
of days or weeks. Perhaps some pain, but no stupefying
drugs. With luck he'd persevere, in his bedroom, until frost
touched upon the manicured ball fields. A season tucked
away in the books. A time to live, and a time to die.

Traps and fishing rights he'd pass on to the Co-op
and they could assign them through a drawing. The coastal
grounds were overfished and not all that much anymore
anyway. Still, it was a pity he didn't have a strong young
son, even a certain daughter to pass things on to, because
it wasn't a bad life and fishing always made comebacks.
Often cold-handed, still you were your own person and
that was worth something—of greater substance than
selling out to bosses up on land. There were fishermen
whose wives conversed with them by shortwave all day,
and much of lobstering depended on luck in your marriage. However solitary you might be on the water, only
a rare bird ever did it successfully alone. Topliners, like
his father, had family support—and wouldn't his father
turn over in his grave if he had seen his son wear that
brown uniform for eight years and slip into being a mar-
ginal fisherman? And Marian, there had been a time when
he thought she'd be a young tomboy daughter to him, a

daredevil daughter, and where had she gone, how had he also lost her to that foul politician?

Yet again Warren sat on the *Lady Bee*'s gunwale, to gather breath and bask in near peace. He wondered what else he should attend to, to avoid leaving anything in a muddle. His assets and insurance all went to Beatrice and to Marian in time. He had no other family—a cousin up around Casco Bay, also working the water—but had never considered leaving anything to anyone other than Beatrice. Nothing large remained that would not take care of itself, he decided, and he used a lobster crate into which to load his personal possessions.

Weapons. He had always kept two aboard, a .22 rifle and, in an oily pouch under lock and key in the pilothouse, his old Colt Python .357 Magnum. He kept the .22 rifle racked in its case under the instrument panel, but did not believe either weapon retained much value and decided to leave the rifle in place for the boat's new owner. Pistol and rifle had been for protection against possible mad dogs and desperadoes at sea—rough traffic did roar into view at times, and turf wars, misunderstandings, and thefts were not unheard of—and also as a means of killing an oversized shark or tuna, should one be brought alongside. In all his years he'd used the rifle to shoot but one tuna, an eight hundred pounder, and maybe ten sharks, but had never had an encounter with a man that led to gunfire.

If he had had the nerve, he thought, or not loved Beatrice as he had, he might have run off and found someone to love him for who he was. But he had not run off, Helen at the diner was long gone in time, and now it was all water under the bridge. He remained attached to his wife—if in devotion or in doglike enslavement, he wasn't sure. He tried to think it out as he lowered an added box and seabag into the dinghy for the last trip to shore. Had he been an ordinary fool? a victim? a man netted? He wished he knew.

The boxes he placed in the truck's bed, the pouch holding the old Python he hefted once, contemplated its power, and placed in the glove box. And as he backed around he thought of the next day's trip to the Co-op as a way to avoid admitting he was turning his back forever on the *Lady Bee*. His boat and life. His everything. If there was a time to not look back, this was it and he maintained eyes front as he rolled away. Dear sweet Jesus. A time to look only ahead.

MARIAN

The sun was a new penny on the horizon and quiet hour was settling over the seacoast and over Maine Authentic. Few evenings were more pleasantly relaxed than weekdays in early October, late in the season for tourists and early for Christmas. Car headlights had been coming on out in the dull air and while the pull was usually to an evening meal—in a restaurant with friends, at home, alone at a counter with a magazine before returning for an evening shift—the pull for Marian tonight (not a very pleasant one) was to call her father, to convey her news and attempt to come to terms with what was happening to him.

She rang up a sale and returned the credit card upside down, glancing to see that one signature resembled the other. It was often this way: the wife making the selection—ceramic candle holders as a wedding gift—the husband producing the plastic and signing the receipt. Husband and wife doing an errand on their way to dinner along the coast. An attractive couple, Marian thought. Not glamorous, but mature and comfortably together. Not an old pair of shoes either, but wool sweater and silk blouse, capable yet of little sparks, content in their intelligent life and lack of problems—the kind of customers her mother loved to serve.

And a way she and Ron would never be, she thought. No matter what good fortune might come their way, sophistication wasn't in the cards for them. Theirs would be yet another spat in his Firebird over driving too fast, over money, over her going alone in her Miata—because she had so come to prefer being by herself to being with him. Yet her anger was not so strong tonight; venting to her mother and Virgil had lifted the cloud she had been carrying, and in fact she was suffering a twinge of betrayal over trashing Ron as she had. He was immature, but he remained her husband.

No other customers were pressing, Lori and John were visible in front, and Marian took the break she had been waiting for. It was close to six and her father would be home from running his traps, while her mother was giving the evening to repositioning the rear woodcraft and pottery sections—in further anticipation of the new line— and would not be leaving until seven-thirty or eight. Conditions were important to Marian: privacy in the office as she called and privacy at home as he received the call. She told Lori she'd be back shortly and remarked to her mother on the way, "I'm going to call Dad," to forestall being followed into the office and hearing a minilecture on the bonding psychology of working late hours together.

Marian punched the numbers she knew from growing up. At the same time, as the telephone rang on Kittery Point, shortcircuits of Ron and herself, of her mother and Virgil, of life and death, even of the middle-class couple she had just served, ran through her mind. She had never disliked her father but for many years she had been unable to love him as she had when she was a child and he picked her up in his truck after school when it was raining, treated her as her best friend, took her on his boat as first mate. Her mother and Virgil had confused everything for her, there was no getting around it. They provided clothes, cars, money, meals out, and, as the years passed, especially after her summer on the boat, distances widened and the air at home grew ever more empty and quiet. In time, at her wedding, there was her father, standing to speak, visibly uneasy, while Virgil, proposing an elaborate champagne toast, was funny and touching and, however long-winded, would have struck strangers as the doting father surrendering his daughter to marriage. There was her own youthful heart, embracing the paternal figure who offered the sweetest and most engaging words, while circumstances compelled her father to stand as little more than a guest.

Still, she loved him—how could she not? Today may have been the first time she had seen how horrible it had to have been for him to have Virgil hovering about his life as he had. Virgil and his power as a politician, from which she had benefited—though even to her it was disturbing to see such influence exerted over another man's family.

Was love to be measured by gifts and a confection of words? by cars and connections? For a time in childhood she had thought Virgil *was* her father, until the blowup about blood testing. Even then she had remained confused, and that her mother assumed all along that she knew the truth had always been a sore point with her. She believed her mother should have clarified things earlier, not when she was eighteen and leaving for college but when she was eleven and told of the school nurse whispering to her teacher in the first-aid room, "Now, who's her father, is it Mr. Hudon, or Mr. Pound?"

"**Aye**?" was how her father answered the phone, as always.

"Daddy, it's me—how are you?"

"Oh, could be better, I guess—how are you, sweetheart?"

"What do you mean—could be better?"

"Oh, I'm fine," Warren said. "Just have this cough—hope it doesn't flare up too much or I won't be able to talk very well."

"You've been to the doctor?"

"I've been—it'll be okay. How are things—are you at work?"

"Daddy, listen, I talked to the Kittery Clinic—I know you're going there for treatment."

"Well, I have been doing that, but things're under control."

"What do you mean—what's under control?"

"Well, they're helping me with this cough. It's coming along."

"Daddy, that's a cancer clinic—do you have cancer?"

"⸻⸻⸻⸻⸻⸻⸻⸻⸻⸻⸻⸻⸻⸻," he said after a moment. "I'm doing okay. You playing detective?"

"They said—I asked for information about what was going on and they said your file says you have no family. Did you tell them that?"

"Honey, listen—I'm taking care of this as best I can. I don't know what their files say."

"Did you say you had no family?"

"I'm not sure what I said."

"Well, will you tell them, when you go back, will you say you have a daughter—and one who cares about you and wants to know what's going on? Can you call them and tell them that?"

"Marian, this has been a hard go, I don't know what to tell you."

"Can't you just say you have a daughter?"

"I can do that. I'll do that."

"Daddy, I'm so sorry the way things have worked out, I really am. I mean, the distance that's grown up between us. It's my fault, I know, and I'm so sorry. I'm sorry you're sick. I feel awful about it."

"Well I do too, Marian, I mean about the distance. It hasn't been the greatest way to live, for sure. Hasn't been anything I wanted. It's been hard."

"Can I come see you?"

"Of course you can. Anytime."

"I don't mean right now, but maybe tomorrow night, after work. Are you still going out every day in your boat?"

"Well, usually, not always these days."

"What I'd like is to talk to the doctor at the clinic, then come see you—maybe around six o'clock tomorrow night—would that be okay?"

"I think so. I'll be here."

"So you're not going out every day?"

"Not as much as I used to. Cough's had me down lately."

"Do you have some kind of cancer?"

"Honey, I don't know. I'll let you know soon as I can."

"Daddy, I have some news—I think it's good news: I'm going to have a baby. I'm over two months along."

"Are you! Now that *is* news. Congratulations—to you and Ron both. That's wonderful news. I'm going to be a grandfather."

She would never speak to her father of her doubts about Ron, certain his response would be different from what she'd heard at lunch, and she said, "I hope I'm up to it."

"Why wouldn't you be? It's wonderful news, Marian. I'm pleased for you, for myself, too. Always wanted to be a grandfather."

"Daddy, you know, I think every day about that summer I went on the boat. It's something that's more important to me all the time. It's one thing we had together."

"That's nice to hear."

"I love it more every day, I really do."

"I do too, sweetheart."

"Daddy, maybe we could use your name in some way, you know, if it's a boy—though I'm pulling for a girl, I have to admit."

"Oh, a little girl would be nice. It was always a surprise, what a treat it was having a little girl."

"You mean a really little girl."

He laughed, even as he coughed. "Of any age," he got out. "As for my name, whatever you do will be fine with me. I'd be flattered, that's for sure, but it's something you better talk over with Ron."

"Daddy, please tell your doctor you have a daughter. Call tomorrow and tell them, will you? Then when I come see you I'll know what's going on. Okay?"

Her father coughed and did not entirely answer, but when Marian replaced the receiver she felt better—felt she would find out at last what was happening to her father as well as to herself. Maybe then, as Virgil had said, she'd begin to be able to deal with it.

Marian lingered in her mother's office, resting her chin on her hands, not wanting to have to explain what her father had had to say. What had he had to say? A bad cough—he wasn't fishing much—he would tell the people at the clinic he had a daughter. Conversations with her father had always been restrained, and the brief exchange she'd just had was as good as it had ever been. He'd never been anything but kind, though for years there had been that widening space between them. She had become, really, her mother's daughter, with a perception of her father that had long ago begun shifting to her mother's side. Then too, Virgil was always kind and loving, always present and more forthcoming with support of all kinds, and also uninhibited with affection and words. She had not intentionally forsaken her father, but was not unaware of what she had done. Her mother's marital deceit was so old it seemed hardly to matter. If only her parents had ended their marriage long ago—what a difference it might have made in all their lives. Maybe her father would have found some happiness. They might have been better friends, too, as father and daughter.

Marian got to her feet, wishing she could deal with Ron in a phone call of the kind. No way. Her pregnancy would elicit no joy or sympathy on that front, she felt certain, and his response would be we-can't-afford-it, your-job-will-have-to-go, your-mother-better-unload-some-bucks-our-way. All the old deep-seated hostility, the shallow land mines in their thirty-month-old marriage. How had she let herself walk wide-eyed into such a hopeless situation?

Well, let him lose his cool, she thought, because nothing would make it easier for her to pack his bag, hand it to him, and show him the door. To think that her feelings for him had fallen so far—not least of all because of yet another immature joke about a bodily function he'd been unable to leave alone for weeks. One thing she knew, she had to tell him soon, because however negative she was feeling it would be unfair—would set off an endless blowup—to have him learn from someone else that he was going to become a father.

Tonight, come what may, she told herself. And let his hostility rear its ugly head, what did she care—for nothing fitted him less than the term father. Father to a six-pack, she thought. To mag wheels and a two-barrel carb. To jokes about cutting the cheese. He who whispered "Hey baby, fuel's on fire" when he wanted to make out. Tonight, she told herself, assuming he came in before midnight.

BEATRICE

Of course he was sick, she could see that now and wasn't going to deny it. His coughing, and avoiding passing her in the house in recent weeks. There was no way, however, that she would be nursing or babying him. If he wanted "no family," let him have it his way. It would be fine with her if he just stayed out of sight. And if he didn't—well, she'd help if he should ask but otherwise she was going to go on as if all were normal. All he was trying to do was get back at her, she thought, and what good was that going to do any of them?

Marian did not seem to have learned much from talking with him on the phone, and here, driving home, Beatrice wished she had taken her daughter out to dinner, to have an added chance to talk things over. Larger things. She felt guilty over the life she had imposed on Marian—but not that guilty; she'd taken a thousand steps toward making her growing up successful, easy, manageable. Friendship, financial support, cars and clothes, a full-blown business to take over. Had any child been dealt the cards she'd been slipping into her daughter's hands?

If anything, Beatrice thought, she should have seen Warren's sickness coming, for what was more inevitable than death? What choice did she have except to survive this season in their life and go on as before? She'd help if she could, and would give comfort to Marian. It was going to be sad, for sure, awful at times, and she was certain Virgil felt the same way—but they wouldn't be turning life upside down to accommodate Warren being sick. They'd do what had to be done, would make things easy for him, and easy for Marian, but the larger picture would be to survive and go on—with precious freedom looming ahead at long last.

She and Warren had a pattern and she wouldn't change that either, unless he asked her to: He did most of the shopping, most of the laundry and house cleaning—none of which he seemed to mind doing, being home many more hours than she—and they rarely crossed paths, only when he was late leaving in the morning because of a low tide or, more rare, when she returned early in the evening from the store, which almost never happened.

More likely, 90 percent of the time, she came home at eight or nine, or ten or later, had a light snack, and retreated to her suite of rooms upstairs to watch TV and putter and plan before going to bed, while he was sleeping or watching TV in his bedroom down the hall. One thing she had made clear years ago was that she had no interest in eating food he might prepare or leave for her. She knew that he wished, in the awful psychology of their relationship, to perform tasks and cook for her, to please her, yet food posed an obligation she could not accept. To eat what he prepared was like sleeping again in the same room or same bed, and the mere thought of intimacy with him repulsed her. She knew he couldn't help himself, but believed also that his state of mind was his to look after. However sorry she was that their life together had turned out as it had, there was nothing she was going to do to change it now.

This cool night, however, and for the first time in a decade and however late, there was a smell of food cooking and it took her by surprise. Seasoned rice, a stir fry with onions—she wasn't sure, but was hungry, and the aroma released an urge in her belly. She had parked beside his pickup and moved across the lighted patio onto the rear deck where a sliding glass door let into the kitchen. The sad frail man was at the stove, and he glanced her way, nodded pleasantly enough while being at once taken with suppressing his cough to the side and could not have spoken if he'd wanted to. No words, no greeting. Life as usual—except that he was preparing food at so late an hour, looked like he wanted to please and speak, and gestured at the frying pan, offering a bite to eat.

Well, why not, Beatrice thought, and on a nod of her own she indicated yes, fine, she'd join him. She had no wish to open a door to his lament (now or ever). Sharing a meal would be sympathy enough for the moment. Passing through to the stairway and upstairs, carrying her shoulder bag, she changed to jeans, sweat shirt, and house shoes, and returned to the kitchen. Vague curiosity and sympathy at the sad-sack sight of him seemed to draw her along. Poor Warren, dear God.

Early on, she'd have to admit, she had loved coming home to warm meals, especially in cool weather after dark. They might have to go back to their first years of marriage to find occasions of Warren, as the first one home, fixing dinner, but it had been their pattern for a time. She enjoyed it for a year or two—his meager cooking skills notwithstanding—but squelched the routine when she sensed his using dinner as a way to control her coming and going. Besides, eating out with associates from state government had become the real fun for her, the action and excitement of the day. Running Virgil's district office had been frantic in those early years, and she hadn't been about to put off persons, projects, or being a player because Warren was home early from fishing and had warned that dinner would be ready to eat at six.

And yes, she had her regrets, things, if given another chance, she would do differently. There was the time she was packing for the Hartford Conference and Warren, home early, entered her bedroom to talk. She had purchased face-powder beige lingerie for the trip—not least of all in anticipation of what she knew the garments would do for Virgil in their hotel room—and had to decide on the spot whether to pack them in Warren's presence or not. Knowing they would taunt him, she removed the garments from tissue paper and placed them in the open suitcase. The perverse teasing made her feel warm inside— then scornful of Warren for failing to respond.

"I hear you're sick—how are you feeling?" she said.

He coughed to the side but there again was something like a smile trying to occupy his face. "Okay," he got out. "I'm okay."

"Marian's pretty worried."

"I have this cough—I'm okay. She's coming to see me."

"She told you about the baby?"

He nodded, said, "I'm happy for her . . . it's nice." Trying once more to smile, he nodded toward the concoction in the frying pan. "Farmer's omelet," he got out.

Beatrice knew by then that he wanted something from her, still the omelet smelled enticing and she decided she'd deal with whatever it was as it came up.

Warren retrieved an egg carton from the refrigerator, and she stood by as he removed a brown shape and cracked it, plop, into a mixing bowl where others waited to be whipped. On the stove in the big Teflon pan was a faintly crackling mix of potatoes, bacon, onions, green pepper, and she said—knowing it may have been the most wifely remark she had offered to him in years—"Anything I can do?"

"Toast?"

Well, her one dietary temptation of the month—not really a rationalization, she thought as she proceeded to make toast and he poured the mix into the pan. Bending away, he coughed again into his fist, but got it under control and resumed his task. "Something we need to talk about," he said.

Well, of course, she thought, but determined not to submit to what she imagined he had in mind, she said, "Do we have to right now—I'm exhausted. Can we put it off for tonight?" He seemed not to respond, and they continued seasoning, buttering, carrying plates to the sun room breakfast table. "I mean, I'm not surprised you want to talk, I figured you did, but it's been a terribly long day— I wouldn't be very good at it right now. How are you feeling?"

He nodded, made an expression. "Maybe it's better we don't do it here anyway. But soon, it'll have to be soon."

"Is there a problem?"

"Well, something I need to tell you, and a favor I want to ask—but they can wait until tomorrow."

"Tomorrow? I don't know about that—I hope you're not serious. I'll be tied up tomorrow, all day long."

"Well—has to be. I won't need much time. No later than tomorrow."

She took a bite, tried to sort through tomorrow in her mind, tried to sort through what was happening. "*When* tomorrow? We're getting into an important new account and I'm really pressed. I understand this is important, or you wouldn't be saying this," she added. "But when, and for how long?"

"Not long," Warren said. "What I'd like is to meet you in a public place, like a coffee shop. Have a cup of coffee. That's all. Coffee and a few words. Or your office, though I know you don't like having me there. Thirty minutes is all, the time of a cup of coffee. Anytime."

Beatrice sighed. "Where is it you're inviting me— exactly?"

"Some place where you'll hear me out. I try to tell you here, you'll close yourself into your room, we both know that." Once again, suppressing his cough, Warren tried to smile.

"Is it that bad—what are you saying?"

"A small favor," he said and coughed. "Won't cost you a thing."

"You're losing me here."

"It's news, something I have to tell you."

"About being sick?"

"Let me say at the time. That's what I'd like to do. I need to think it out, and I have a couple things yet to do, tomorrow. I just want to ask a small favor of you, that's all."

"Warren, I'm tired—but I'll hear you out right now if you like."

"Tomorrow would be better. I have to sort out what I want to say."

"What I'm saying is that I don't know about tomorrow. We're busy with this new account, it's extremely important, the biggest thing we've ever done, and I won't have time to slip away for thirty minutes, which always means an hour. I just won't have time for that."

"It's just a small favor. Thirty minutes, that's all."

"What's the subject? Is it your sickness?"

"I want to tell you when I tell you."

"You fixed this meal to paint me into a corner, didn't you?" she said, trying to appear amused. "I guess it worked. Nearly worked."

"Lost my appetite long ago," Warren got out and, as if she were a stranger, tried once more to send a relic of a smile her way. "It's nothing you'll mind hearing," he said. "Just a small favor. Sort of a peace pipe is what it is."

The pathetic man, Beatrice said to herself as she retreated upstairs. His life had been a misery and the blame fell squarely on her, there was no getting away from it. She had thought hundreds of times how happy he could have been with any other woman, and how easy it would have been, twenty-five years ago, to have cut him loose. Of course it wouldn't have been easy for Virgil, and that was the nub that Warren had never put together: A key female aide, divorced (and involved with her boss), could have destroyed Virgil politically if word had gotten out. Warren had to be tolerated for appearances, a circumstance of which he appeared to remain endlessly unaware. At the same time it weighed on her conscience and made her cringe every time she thought of it. Complimented for niceness, liveliness—often for loyalty, though to her boss— her guilt thrived within. The worst part was using Warren for cover down through the years while knowing it was a form of torture. He had spent his life thrashing, neither dead nor alive; she had spent hers looking the other way.

Now Marian was having problems in *her* young marriage and Beatrice thought that no matter the Church or any temporary inconvenience, she'd support divorce all the way. Nothing, unless it was something as substantial as her own store, would be worth the guilt and unhappiness that surfaced everyday. Getting ready for bed, she recalled a time last winter when she had suffered yet another nightmare over Warren—one that clung to her throughout an entire day—and how she had tried, inviting Marian for a late bite to eat, to confess to her the dilemma with which she had lived most of her life. Who else than your best friend to whom to bare your stricken soul?

Her confession took a surprising turn, however, as Marian came up less than sympathetic. Dry snow was blowing, and on an invitation to join her after work, Beatrice led her to one of the high-walled booths at Cafe Balderacchi in Portsmouth where, speaking of Warren, she soon confessed that she feared she was torturing him, that he appeared to be suffering mental anguish, that she herself had been losing sleep over it. To her surprise, Marian did not argue to the contrary, did not say her father's problems had been of his own making, as Beatrice had anticipated, but said, "I'm sure it *has* been torture for him, especially with the store catching on as it has."

Vaguely hurt, Beatrice took a moment. "You think I have tortured him?"

Marian made an expression more yes than no.

"I guess it's true," Beatrice said at last.

"He's had his lobstering business," Marian offered.

"I've damaged him, I know I have. I've never wanted to admit it to myself."

"Mother, he's had a life," Marian said.

"I'd give anything to believe that was true—I know it isn't."

After a moment Marian said, "No one ever made him do anything he didn't want to."

"What I wouldn't give to believe that," Beatrice said.

WARREN

In his bedroom down the hall he had turned on the TV and was sitting in a chair, gazing more within than without. Having a meal with Beatrice was unheard of and his hopes felt up for the favor he wanted to ask: that they forgo their terrible past, that she and Virgil shake hands with him and agree that life hadn't turned out to be what any of them had thought it would be, and fare thee well . . . that he might lie back in peace, watching the World Series and sinking into eternity.

Otherwise Warren had little idea of what to expect in the coming days. He knew only that he was failing fast and had no wish to lose his place next to his wife in the hereafter. However long it might take to occur he hoped ultimately to be with her along the expanse that lay ahead. If he was trying to put anything over on her, it was only to gain the peace of mind that forgiveness might bring, to avoid alienating himself on the infinite journey ahead.

Sitting with her at the table had been pleasant if bittersweet. They had done things together on occasion—not unlike other couples—but Warren had to strain to recall the last occasion: a town meeting several years ago to hear an appeal for variance to convert property near the town green to commercial parking. Married property owners each had a vote—as they had been reminded in a campaign of calls and fliers—and he and Beatrice joined other residents to hear the debate and to voice yea or nay. The parking scheme was objectionable even to independent fishermen—larger devaluation of the town devalued everything—and being rallied to a common cause had afforded them the occasion of doing something together. Then the meeting itself turned into a surprising if modest celebration: greeting lifelong acquaintances, climbing onto bleacher seats, seeing who had aged, who had prospered. They looked like any other Kittery couple, Warren thought, until the vote was taken and it was time to make their way outside. Beatrice, popular as always, was signaled by smiles and words all along, as he trailed a few steps behind, though he also smiled once or twice, fooling himself that all was well and life had yet to make its irreversible turn. But as they exited the building she turned with her keys—they'd come in her car—and asked if he minded driving home, she needed to talk mall business with Grant and Karina and would have them drop her off.

Warren's heart sank but he could only say he didn't mind. Why should he—hadn't their evening out been merely an accident? But as she left, engaged in ongoing chatter along the path of a summer night, an image of their life from beginning to end gripped him and he had to pause in shadows to steel himself against raging into madness. He wanted not to be alive, wanted to hurt her, and his impulse that forlorn night was to drive home, attach a hose to her car's exhaust, and leave his remains in the driveway to be found by her on her return. As it ended up, he drank himself into a stupor and when he awakened at the kitchen table she was already home and locked in her room upstairs.

Lapsed Catholic or not—neglectful more than expired—Warren's growing belief was that the world would go on forever and would somehow take him along. He had been searching his beliefs here in adulthood: If one were not lost into oblivion—the fate of suicides, mortal sinners, nonbelievers—might there not be a hereafter, perhaps in a form of one's mind continuing to exist? In time, other minds would join that greater sea of consciousness sailing through eternity, and Beatrice would arrive and fall in beside him. His self-loathing over his failures with her, over having worked as a lackey for her boss and lover, would be as nothing in that ultimate universe. They would sail on as husband and wife, in the eyes of their creator and beyond flesh and aging. All they had been taught as children would prove to be so, and they would be as children once more and throughout all time.

The vision encouraged Warren's damaged heart, at the same time that it raised a hollow feeling in his throat. It had come to this. He was gaining faith in faith, while craving death, he knew, as one craves a fatal storm gathering on the horizon. Take me unto Thee, he thought. Oh Lord, let me be free in Thee at last.

Warren was not a reader or writer of letters, but he had a notion to write a note indicating his condition, to leave it for her to find in the morning after he had left the house— to prepare her and remind her that he would be calling to arrange a time to meet. Thus did he return downstairs, to use stationery they kept in a cupboard there:

Dear Beatrice,

This is to let you know that my days are numbered.
Call Dr. Dawson if you want to. He did X ray,
biopsy, and so forth. He said it is oat cell cancer
which explains the cough. He can't say how much
time is left but it could be days which is why I need
to talk to you right away. What I'd like is to have us
make up. I want that more than anything. I don't
mean in every way, only as friends so I can know
some peace at last. I've been your husband all these
years. I want you to be happy. I want Virgil and
Marian to be happy. I won't ask for anything more.

Love,
Warren

TWO

BEATRICE

At daybreak she heard Warren's truck drive away and experienced the relief she felt every time he left the house. During the night she had thought about his wanting to talk and had grown increasingly suspicious. The news had to be his health—more than thin, he looked frail—at the same time she couldn't help sensing he was trying to manipulate her. Meeting in a "public place" felt ominous to her. True, she had occasionally retreated to her room, but did he really think she would not sit through his "news"? A public place? It sounded like those awful crime stories they report on TV.

Above all she felt burdened with guilt and responsibility. He remained her husband and if it were up to her she'd have him live a hundred years, and in good health. He had been the one to suffer, after all, and the last thing she wanted was to see him suffer more.

Brushing and washing in her bathroom, rubbing in lotions, she recalled the time when he was too sick with pneumonia to go to work and she felt obligated, as his wife, to care for him. To his credit he tried to make her task as minimal as possible. She was running Virgil's district office at the time and though she could take time off, Warren knew she didn't really want to and—when she had been home an hour past her usual departure time and had ordered medicine by phone—he asked her to please leave and let him take care of himself.

In time he told her she was making him feel worse and insisted she leave. He said he couldn't stand the idea of her resenting waiting on him. For her part, she said she wouldn't do it if she resented it, and when he told her to please go, she paused awhile longer, fixed him soup and drove to Laverdiere's for the medicine. It was a curious experience for her, driving away, as she re-called the strength about him that had appealed to her years earlier, and why they had married. It was the same mix of guilt with which she had lived throughout her first decade or so of being with Virgil: knowing in her heart that she and Warren could have built a life together. They would have had more children and—who knew?—in time he might have been running half a dozen boats, making good money, and she'd have been at the center of life on shore as a topliner's wife and business man-ager. A solid citizen in town. From the vantage point of how things had gone the thought was bittersweet, be-cause she knew it could have happened had she given it her best. Warren was not bad at heart, and they would have been happy with their clambakes, cookouts, children, and community life. They would have succeeded, because she would have made it happen; it had been her dream in the first place, when she selected shy, gangly Warren as her husband, back in eleventh grade, when she had bought into the idea of being a good woman behind a successful man.

How astonishing that she had ended up as the other woman in a powerful politician's life. How strange the turns of fate. She guessed there were scores of women like herself out there, companions of attractive, influential men, but she didn't think it was a career any of them had studied for or anticipated. Though they could have; the role wasn't that unusual.

Cup of coffee in hand, she found Warren's note on the sun room table. Oat cell cancer. Dear God, she thought as she read it, though it wasn't really a surprise. His words filled her heart and eyes, but she knew—also in her heart—that his news wasn't entirely bad, that she was going to be free of the burden of him at last. He would know peace, too, and even as she would have her guilt to manage, she would finally have a life all her own to plan and manage. She had only to survive the coming weeks, an uncertain season, and help him as best she could, though she knew he'd insist on doing everything his own way.

WARREN

Another day. He savored it like a dollar to spend in childhood. How surprising it was to appreciate something as ordinary as the song his tires sang crossing the bridge into Portsmouth. That and the music of foghorns and shrieking gulls, the bell of the old bridge rising on the half hour to admit a freighter or high-masted sail boat. Life's dime-a-dozen pleasures, now that the sale was ending.

He did not go to the *Lady Bee* though he felt the pull at the intersection where he always turned in the direction of Narrow Cove. She would stand at anchor until someone took her over, and even then her days of outlasting rough seas were hardly better than his own. Over Memorial Bridge, at the waterfront diner facing the harbor, opposite the naval shipyard, he sat at the counter as always and knew that a fuse was burning within, knew yet again that he had to win in this final test of wills with Beatrice. After their first years of marriage, when things had gone bad, he had lost every issue to come up between them. He knew that his need to have his way was making him frantic—he recalled his youthful desire to win—and urged himself to call up any possible expedience or guile. *For once in your life make something work with her,* he kept telling himself. *Impress her with your perseverance.*

The challenge: to remain above her disdain and allow her to be the open-hearted person he knew her to be—if only long enough to hear his appeal. Hadn't he glimpsed her good side last night, sitting at the table? There were reasons she was well liked, reasons Virgil was entangled with her. She was smart, generous, energetic. She had always been pretty. And sexy. And wasn't her resenting him but an outgrowth of the guilt his presence had to make her feel? He believed it was. The only time he had deserved her wrath was when he forced the blood test on their daughter, to confirm once and for all that she too did not belong to that squid of a politician who counted so much else of York County among his holdings.

In time—when she would have read his note and left for the store—he'd call and ask to meet for coffee as soon as possible and wherever she liked. Then—as he was still sorting it out in his mind—he'd tell the truth, that he was sorry their life had turned out as it had, was sorry for his part, that there was nothing to do about it now, and say that all he wanted was to shake hands and say "Farewell, I'll see you on the other side."

He would not reveal his wish that they lie next to each other throughout eternity. At the same time, spiritual existence was becoming his belief, if it came from long-ago catechism or not. Ultimate companionship. Year after year, husband and wife. Virgil would be elsewhere with his own wife, and in a generation or two no one would connect their names ever again. It was Warren's final dream: sailing through time, a pair that had become one in marriage and, though severely tested, had never been put asunder. After all, they were husband and wife.

Rockabilly was playing, cigarette smoke joined an indoor cloud of bacon and home fries, and his cough—as, inexplicably, it did now and then—had fled (but for the sandpaper of cancer draping his esophagus like a colony of bats). He had no appetite for anything but coffee, and wondered why he should find hope in a butt-littered waterfront diner never visited by the likes of Beatrice or Virgil Pound. But wasn't it the way of Jesus, in stories from the Bible? *For God so loved the world . . .* Warren's faith felt all the more real and he sensed his mother, on high, being pleased.

Was this heavenly diner a place to which to invite Beatrice—if she could find a place to park among the pickups, motorcycles, and clunkers lined up outside? No, there was no way she'd come here, and the last thing she'd do, should he offer, would be to ride in his pickup—though there had been a time when nothing had thrilled her more. What a sad mix they had turned out to be. Why hadn't someone intercepted them in high school and given them the word?

Well, because they wouldn't have listened, Warren thought.

And if he had failed to grow, had been possessive as she had charged, or if the problem was her abandoning ship, he wasn't sure. Maybe they had just pulled in opposite directions. All he knew with certainty was that they had joined as one, had remained under the same roof, and that his resentment was gone now and he longed to offer forgiveness—to know peace and be together with her in the hereafter. The alternative was oblivion—an ache of never-ending aloneness. It was an ache life had taught him so well he wanted to be free of it at any cost. Nothing had ever hurt him as thoroughly as had aloneness.

At the house, climbing from his truck next to where her car had been parked—a space as haunting as other things about her he'd been unable to touch or hold—he wondered if she might surprise him with a note, or a message on the answering machine. Not likely, he thought, as he entered the house through the sliding glass door. He had said he'd call her, and in spite of the sickness he had confessed in his letter, wouldn't she assume he'd gone to work and would call her from the Co-op?

So it was: no surprising note or blinking red light. The old hollow disappointment. But then why would she accommodate him now when she had never done so before? And even if she were pained over his being under attack by that fastest multiplying of carcinogenic barracudas—wouldn't she be happy to be getting rid of him at last? He didn't blame her. Who wouldn't sense relief at the departure of a burdensome mate? someone you had betrayed and over whom you suffered guilt? No, he understood and did not blame her.

Still, feeling as anxious as a boy calling a girl for a date, he dialed Maine Authentic. He'd clean up and shave and meet her wherever she cared to meet. "It's her husband," he said to the woman who answered, and when Beatrice came on, he said, "It's me, calling to set up a time and place."

"Warren, I was so sorry when I read your note. I can't tell you—it makes me feel awful. I'm happy you called."

"Well, there it is. There's nothing to be done about it."

"There's no treatment?"

"Nothing that would do any good."

"Is that what Dr. Dawson said?"

"I could get treatment but he didn't say it would do any good. It just makes you miserable for a longer time. It's too far gone."

Upon a pause, she said, "You're at the Co-op?"

"I'm at home. What I'd like is to meet you, say for a cup of coffee. Anywhere. I won't bother you again after that. Just twenty or thirty minutes—it won't have to take an hour."

"Warren, how long have you known? You sure there's nothing that can be done?"

"I've known awhile, I guess, a few weeks. I knew, but I didn't know."

"You could have done something—is that what you're saying?"

"Just chemicals, get some more days is all. To what purpose? I'd rather have my wits about me for what time I have. I'd rather talk to you for half an hour—I'd like that more than a month being full of chemicals and feeling awful."

"Warren—how can you know how many days you'd get from treatment? I don't understand that."

"Please, let me do this my way. You go through phases—which is what I've been doing. My whole life, with you, has been going through phases. This is the last one. I know what I'm doing."

"Well, I'm sorry you feel like you do. I am sorry."

"All I want is to meet with you and ask a small favor. That's all. Bring Virgil, if you want to. I just want to ask a small favor, of both of you, then I'd like to settle in and watch the World Series. That's all I'm asking, nothing more."

"Well, what else did the doctor say?"

"If you mean how long—he said he can't say. He said it could be weeks, even days, I guess. I'm okay with it, I'm settling it out."

"Warren, God—this is awful."

"Well—I guess that's nice of you to say. Is there a place we can meet—can we do it right away so I can have it done with?"

"You want to ask a favor?"

"A small favor—it won't cost you a thing."

"It doesn't have to do with Marian, does it?"

"Nothing like that. Just something sentimental." Warren covered his mouth as he coughed. "A last small request," he said and coughed.

"You can't just say what it is?"

"Well—what it is, what it is is that you meet with me so I can say it. That's all. I want to meet with you. One last time."

"But what is it—you can't just tell me?"

"It would sound foolish if I said it over the phone. What I'd like, is to have a look in your eye and say what I have to say. A small favor—in a public place. Twenty minutes of your time, nothing more."

"A public place—what does that mean exactly?"

"A diner, a coffee shop, that's all, something like that."

"Do you know how that sounds—a public place? It sounds frightening—like something you see on TV or read in the paper."

He could sense from her voice that her guard was up and she wasn't about to give in. "There's nothing to worry about. It's just an expression."

"Warren, you know, I'm going to have to think this over. It makes me uncomfortable. I don't see why you can't just tell me what it is, so I can tell you how I feel about it to begin with."

Warren sensed losing to her yet again, but tried not to show it in his voice. "It's not a big thing," he got out, evenly.

"Warren, I'm sorry you're sick. I'm sorry your life has gone like it has. But you're trying to get me to do something I don't want to do—and it makes me uncomfortable. I just don't like the sound of meeting in a public place. I don't know who would."

"You name the place. It's just an expression, good Lord."

"You can't say what it is?"

"Just to talk for a few minutes. I can't do it on the phone!"

Upon another pause she said, "I have to think about this. You're at home?"

"I told you I was."

"How long will you be there?"

"You can't give me fifteen minutes of your time?" His voice cracked with disappointment.

"Don't you see how threatening it is to have someone talk like you're talking? You think about telling me what you want, over the phone—or when I come home, though I'll be running late tonight. Warren, this isn't easy—it makes me awfully tense, and I'm extremely busy here. Whatever the circumstances, I can't just take time off."

"You'll call back?"

"In a while! I have to think about this. Warren, I'm sorry you're sick—but it's like you're trying to rake me over the coals! I can't let you do that, I'm sorry."

The dial tone came before Warren could ask if she wanted him to beg. The hum left him sinking in hopelessness. Was he asking so much? Did she think he was going to grab a knife like that football player? Couldn't she see that he only wanted to get through to her, to them, for a moment, to take a measure of hope and peace of mind, a measure of her affection, into whatever lay ahead?

MARIAN

Arriving late, she was aware that a call had come from her father and wasn't surprised when her mother buzzed the desk and asked her to come to the office. Meeting her and closing the door behind her—that in itself was unusual—her mother avoided eye contact and Marian was uncertain if she should sit or stand. Something in her mother's manner reminded Marian of being a schoolgirl and the acrimony between her parents being heartrending in ways she was never able to shed. During all those growing-up years, going to catch the bus from a household in which emotions were so angry left her frightened and anxious over returning home at the end of the day.

"You don't have to worry about calling his doctor—your father told me he has terminal lung cancer. He left a note this morning and he just called."

"Oh God, I knew it was something like that," Marian said.

"I guess it's what he wanted. I asked him but he wouldn't tell me anything."

"It's awful—and I feel responsible. His life's been horrible, and now this."

Marian choked; all she could get out was, "He said he wanted to be a grandfather."

"Well, I always hoped he might find some happiness in his life," her mother said. "It never happened." She was teary-eyed, too, and they more or less embraced. "'No family.' What he wants is to make us feel bad."

"Did he say how long?"

"He said the doctor said weeks, maybe days—I guess it's a fast-growing cancer." Then her mother said, "He's all worked up about a favor he wants to ask me, only he won't say what it is—unless I meet him in a public place."

"Unless you do what—what does that mean?"

"It sounds threatening to me—does it to you?"

"You mean like in a park or something?"

"No, a coffee shop, or a diner, is what he said. He told me to invite Virgil, said he wanted to speak to both of us."

"Don't do it, is what I'd say. It sounds strange, I don't like the sound of that. He wasn't like that when I talked to him."

"It does sound strange—that's what I keep thinking."

"Have you told Virgil?"

"I will. It's all just happened. He left the note this morning, and I just got off the phone from talking to him."

"Well, you shouldn't be meeting him in a public place. That's what I'd say. And he won't do treatment—he said that?"

"He won't have anything to do with it—wants to get back at me, I'm sure."

They stood sniffling, shaking their heads, using Kleenex.

"I'm surprised he went to a doctor at all," Beatrice said, and added, "I don't mind granting him a favor—but I don't see why he can't tell me what the subject is over the phone."

"It's hard to know what he might be thinking."

"I've treated him so badly. That's what's awful for me. I couldn't have treated him more badly."

"Mother, don't say that."

"I could have cut him loose a long time ago. He'd have been a lot happier."

"You can't live your life over again—you're the one always saying that."

"The problem is, I knew what to do, and so did Virgil—only we didn't do it. Virgil's career would have been threatened and we never wanted to face it."

Her mother embraced her again, wept into her hair: "You're the one I've loved. You're the best friend a person could have. I mean that. You're the one I've worked for."

Marian returned to the floor but twenty minutes later was back in the office to be with her mother. "I feel like I should do something, but I don't know what to do," she said. "I can't just go back to work."

"If I had it to do over again, I'd never get married," her mother said. "I'd have you as my daughter but I wouldn't be getting married."

"You don't mean that—but I do," Marian said and they laughed some in their gasping and sniffling.

"All I've ever wanted was to leave something nice for you," Beatrice said. "That's all I've wanted. For my daughter, and my grandchildren. I'm sure I'd feel the same if I'd had a son. Virgil has meant the world to me, and there was a time, believe it or not, when I was crazy about your father. But what became important to me was to leave something nice for you. That's what I've worked for. Every time I've worked late, or done something hard, I've told myself I was doing it for you and your children—not that you have to feel obligated, because you don't."

Marian stood there teary-eyed, and Beatrice came up with more tissues with which to press and daub. Knowing all along that one of them should be on the floor, Marian soon dropped hers in the waste basket and said, "I'll get back," and added, "Mom, I love you."

"Honey, I love you so much," her mother said and hugged her again. "I'll talk to your father—and see if there's anything we can do. But I don't think I'll be meeting him."

Lori was checking out a young guy while a crowd of customers waited, and, moving into place at the other end of the counter, Marian nodded to say she was open. At the same time she could not get her father out of her mind. Didn't he need friendship, especially now? She recalled fifth grade, when sharp words had intensified at home—stabbing into many nights over several weeks—and the day her father removed her from school and drove her in his pickup to the Maine Medical Center in Portland where, for reasons unknown to her, a needle was slipped into her arm and vials of blood taken. A decade passed before she learned that a paternity test had been performed, which determined she was not the child of her mother's boss, but of the man identified all along as her father. No one explained anything to her at the time, however, and through seventh and eighth grades—when she spent an abundance of time around him and he was so kind and attentive—had believed the opposite, that the prominent state senator, the man whose picture was often in the paper, was her actual father. The truth was something she came to believe her mother should have clarified to her, even if doing so would have been to confirm what was apparently obvious. Her mother liked to say she was her best friend—who else to clarify something of the kind?

In her own mind—at the time—Marian went from first mate to being the secret child of the man who dressed in dark suits and was driven in long black cars with Maine Legislature license plates. From a summer on a lobster boat to summers in an air-conditioned office and in large cool cars wherein to say "Hey, Jude" to her make-believe girl-friend. She carried out a daughter's love affair with one father, then with another, and only later saw that she too had forsaken one for the magnetic appeal of the other, that her father had faded in her eyes while the senator and state liquor commissioner had grown warmer, fun-nier, ever easier to talk to than the staunch figure who all but lived on a littered and stinky boat.

By then it was too late to turn back, wasn't it—when her father was so distant and floating farther away?

If only she had *not* known in her heart's core that it wasn't too late at all, that she had been making choices for wealth and privilege, for clothes, jewelry, makeup. But she had known all along, and suffered over it still; it was what she was knowing again today as she served custom-ers and tried to smile through filmed-over eyes. At the time she had persuaded herself that her mother was at the helm of her existence—that she was merely a girl and too young to know the difference: A boy might be expected to stand with his father in such a crisis, but not a girl, wasn't it so? Wasn't a girl at the mercy of powerful men in whose presence she found herself, should she be so fortunate? Weren't powerful men the answer to a girl's dreams? She did not feel that way now, but in adolescence it had appeared to be the way of the world, and the way of all flesh, not excluding her own.

VIRGIL

He returned the Thomaston file to the Maine Authentic drawer and decided to treat himself to a brandy, though it was hardly ten a.m. Not that the hour mattered. Virgil liked inventing his own rules, however quietly he might do so. As he always thought, stealth has its advantages. It might not be a strategy they teach in business school (just as well, else it wouldn't be stealth), but alas, let the race be to those who accumulate the marbles while others pay fees and rates.

Things were falling into place and Virgil was feeling ever more bold this morning. There was the Warren business to suffer through but he wouldn't be letting it get under his skin and it would pass. One more call—just to be certain—then he'd leave to be with Beatrice when the call came from the bank. But first the brandy (and another, if he felt like it) because he was certain the bank would carry the note. How could they not? Everyone would benefit and the strings were neatly tied. York National would make money, he and Beatrice would make money, and the note would be paid off in five years—while the contract with the state (to be sure) was renewable. A no-lose deal all the way around. He had stitched it together himself just before leaving office, and the key innovation was that note and contract would be held by Beatrice. She would be entirely on her own and would fly ever higher. Could anyone have had a more successful apprentice, or been more fulfilled as a mentor? Besides all else she was to him Beatrice was like a fond offspring being handed the reins of a family enterprise. Virgil admired legendary families that built empires lasting generations, and only wished, here in his own senior years, that their names were the same. Had fate been on their side, he and Beatrice would be priming children of their own to assume roles in such a family. Imagine the lineage they might have produced. That it wasn't so was one of his deepest disappointments.

His offices were above Kittery Pizza on Route 1 with a wall of canopied windows framing a wide-angled view of Portsmouth Harbor and the Route 1 Memorial Bridge to the south. The offices might be described as modest at

best. But for the graphite Mercedes in the four-space lot
outside, the view of the wide river mouth between Maine
and New Hampshire was the only suggestion of privilege,
though the square footage—above an aromatic pizza par-
lor or not—might appear excessive for what Virgil occasionally referred to as a one-man operation.

One man and one or two extraordinary women, he
thought, sipping his drink and gazing over his small corner of the world. Give him an extraordinary woman every
time, as a secret weapon. It was immigrants in the past,
now it was women surfacing after having been suppressed
for years. Ordinary looking, dedicated, smart. More than
just willing, they worked three times as hard as others.
That was Beatrice, for sure, though for the moment he
was thinking of Janet Derocher, presently in the outer
office with its lesser view of Route 1 and the seafood
wholesaler across the road. Janet was also worth her
weight in gold. They were women of such competence
and personality that, set loose, they could compete with
the cream of the crop in any brand-name corporation. (Not
Marian, he was afraid, nor his wife or daughters, nor most
of the women coming and going in the world around
them.) Still, there was an untapped resource in those who
were gifted because men, and women, too, had for so long
measured them through narrow lenses. They were women
who were often modest and unaware themselves of the

gifts with which they had been blessed. The self-important among them usually proved foolish, while the diamonds-in-the-rough, the Beatrices and Janets, were usually self-effacing. Stealth and boldness were rarely in their quivers, and maybe there was a reason for the glass ceiling, but pound for pound those certain unassuming women would leave many executives scrambling to add up yesterday's bottom line. It was a little secret that wasn't necessarily dirty and one he should point out to Beatrice for the future—though how might he do so without indicating her own daughter might not have the goods? (Unless he was wrong about Marian, which he wished he was.)

Champagne—of course! He'd sneak a bottle into the store and when the call came from the bank he'd rally Marian, and others, and toast Beatrice for gaining the unique new inventory. What could be more authentic, he'd say, than hand-crafted breadboards, toys, salad bowls, bagel racks, laminated birdhouses and utensils made of pine, spruce, cedar, and made—exclusively—within the Maine state prison system! Who could *be* more authentic than Beatrice Hudon with her exclusive contract!

She'd be thrilled by a champagne toast and deserved to be, Virgil thought. It was an amazing coup and would bring in thousands down through the years. Tens of thousands. The ash/maple, red/blond bookends alone would become heirlooms and it was clear already that customers would not be able to resist what Beatrice was calling "melodies in wood grain carved by the hands of stricken souls."

On the telephone with Jay Shute, Virgil liked how the young banker addressed him: "Senator, the board gave unanimous approval without hesitation." Virgil gave a little fist pump with his free hand.

"Mr. Shute, could you do me a small favor?" he asked. "Wait forty minutes before you call Mrs. Hudon with the news. I'd like to be there for a little celebration when the call comes in. Then, sometime after lunch, we'll pick up the paperwork. This is something she's worked hard for."

"No problem, Senator. I'll call Mrs. Hudon at eleven, how would that be?"

"Excellent."

Life can be a treat, Virgil thought as he inventoried his schedule before leaving. Do your work, maintain your mind-set, keep your ducks in a row—have sense enough to enjoy small successes—and life can be a bowl of truffles. He finished his second brandy, rinsed the glass in the adjoining washroom, and told Janet on the way out that he should be back by around three-thirty. "Remind me to give you a raise before the end of the year—would you?" he said.

Her face angled his way. "Mr. Pound, thank you."

"You deserve it. Every investment and property on the books is looking great this year and it's due in no small part to your sharp eye."

"That is nice to hear."

"After the first of the year we'll get you started in some accounts of your own, so you can be building a future, too."

"I'd like that, Mr. Pound. Thanks for thinking of me like that. I'd like that a great deal."

"Want to keep you around," Virgil said, on which note, smiling, he closed the door and went on his way. He certainly did want to keep her around, he thought as he clipped down the outdoor stairway. As with Beatrice, few things gave him so much satisfaction anymore as having a hand in someone catching on in life. Especially a woman coming into awareness of untapped skills and intelligence—another of his little secrets that was in no way dirty. In twenty years' time Janet could be on her own, too, and down through the years everyone in her family might realize the benefits of her industry and good sense.

Given the luck of a certain mentor, he reminded himself.

Spotting Marian behind a cash register, Virgil entertained his old doubts about her. He saw her try to smile at an oblivious customer and realized she was half-stricken. Noticing him, she indicated with a nod that her mother was in the office to the rear. The time of the call from the bank was ten minutes away and Virgil signaled to Marian to confer with him to the side, while a thought entering his mind was to bypass Marian altogether—her problems were already wearying—and proceed with the toasting of her mother on his own. He didn't; without making eye contact, looking past her hair, he told of the loan going through, the call being on its way and, indicating his parcel, having champagne with which to make a toast. "Imported," he said.

"She'll love that," Marian said. "Only there's something else that has to be dealt with—but it's okay."

Virgil knew at once that it had to be more news of Warren, and his heart sank. "Did you talk to the doctor?"

"He's got lung cancer. He may have only weeks or days. He's done nothing. No, I haven't talked to the doctor."

"You all right?"

"I'm trying, I'm doing okay."

"It's that far along? How's your mother doing?"

Marian made an expression and Virgil could see a darkness in her eyes from weeping. "She's okay," Marian said. "I'm supposed to see him tonight—maybe I'll get a better handle on what's happening."

"Well, the account's gone through—I have this champagne for a little celebration. Should we go ahead with it? It may be awkward timing but it's something your mother's worked on for two years."

"We should do it. As for my father, he wants to meet with her, to ask some favor—to meet with you, too, I guess—and she's worried."

"Well, let's do what we have to do. C'mon back in a minute and we'll drink a little toast. You didn't tell Ron?" he added.

Marian shook her head, appearing undone by the question, and Virgil patted her shoulder. "Poor thing, you've had a lot coming your way, haven't you," he said.

WARREN

He recalled the first time she stayed away overnight, and, to his surprise, humiliation and anger rose in him again. He had no wish to reopen the old wound but was helpless against its unfolding. That was his problem—helplessness where she was concerned. She came right at him that first time with what she was doing, said she imagined it would upset him and if so, it was his problem and she was sorry. They were going to Augusta for the state liquor commissioner's hearings and would be staying overnight—the hearings would not conclude until late afternoon of the third day when she would return home by ten or eleven p.m.

Why did she have to do this to him? he had wanted to know.

It was the senator's best chance to gain the position, and he needed his administrative assistant with him to help with documents, paperwork, inquiries. It was her job, was what she was paid to do.

How did Abby feel about her husband staying overnight in Augusta with his administrative assistant?

That she didn't know, it wasn't any of her business.

Would she and Virgil have meals together?

Probably, some of the time, teamwork was essential.

Including breakfast?

Why not—the day's agenda had to be prepared.

Would they be sleeping together? Warren asked, while in his mind he envisioned them in a hotel room locked together.

Don't be ridiculous, she said to him.

Did she know that some people in town believed they were a couple of long standing—she and Virgil?

There was nothing she could do about what people wanted to believe. That was their problem.

Was she in love with Virgil? Warren had said and his head had buzzed as he waited for her to reply.

Virgil was her best friend. She worked for him. That was all she could say.

That sounded like yes to him.

He could hear what he wanted, she didn't care.

Go then, he told her. Let your conscience be your guide.

She wasn't asking his permission to do her job.

He said nothing more, and she walked from the house, slamming the door. Knowing in his bones that more was in place than friendship between his wife and her boss, he tried to gaze away from what he knew. He hoped she had Virgil on a leash, too, but whenever he gave the thought any room, he knew it couldn't be so. Virgil was a person who lived to have his way, and deep down Warren guessed he may have been exciting to her precisely because he refused to submit. And years later, when he overheard on a dock above where he stood in his boat, "Well, at least Senator Pound and *his secretary* don't waste state funds on separate rooms," followed by laughter, he was wounded all over again, though not surprised.

Half an hour, he thought she had said. It seemed that an hour had passed and, big surprise, there had been no call. Had she treated anyone, ever, the way she treated him? Still, something within him was finding perverse satisfaction in her response and he tried without success to envision what he might do if she wouldn't hear him out. Did he *desire* that moral outrage be on his side?

Retreating to the sun room, Warren urged himself not to panic and to take solace in what he had. He was alive, could think and remember things. Pain was close— a platter of water carried in both hands, threatening to spill, a cornhusk of a windpipe threatening to split open within—and existed mainly in the threat of coming up unable to breathe or move. Suffocation and paralysis, a loss of control—they were his sources of fear. It might take hours to die, and he wondered if one resurfaced at once within another world. If he had a soul, would it be swimming all at once within a space like the one he had been imagining? Was a soul but a speck of plankton in the kingdom of the sea—or was it nothing more than an ancient dream?

In the sun room, through the window, Warren watched squirrels in their adept ways preparing for winter. He admired squirrels for their orderly life, their quick moves and speed. Squirrels would make perfect infielders, devouring ground balls, digging them out and executing double plays. Stealing bases, coming in standing up, they would eclipse the immortals.

At least he could think of things. He could visit past and present, and add up one thing and another. That morning, as always, he had wanted to be away from the house before Beatrice started her morning routine. Like a child playing hooky, he had wanted her to think he was at work. Now, at home, it was like missing school as a child, waiting for the telephone to ring. Clouds were moving and there was added light in the room—a thin light overall, though still a balmy day for baseball in October. He realized he both loved and hated his wife. He wanted to make her happy and wanted to hurt her for what she had done to him. He should have left her long ago when she first took up with Virgil. To think he had worn the horns as if forever, had worn that brown uniform and cap, had carried an ache of loneliness and avoided intercourse with people because he knew they knew. Every day he had felt humiliated. What a fool's parade his life had been.

Time was racing—now that so little was left to him. Why wouldn't she just see him? Did she have to confer with her other husband, which was what Virgil was in all but name? Had he *possessed* her as Warren himself had not? In bed, had she curled in under his arm and been his girl and his wife of the heart? Was it a question he dared ask, if she agreed to meet with him? He knew if he asked such a question at home she'd turn away and close herself into her room. But didn't he deserve to hear an answer as the game of life was coming to an end?

Well, don't get bent out of shape ahead of time, he told himself. *Your lungs are going and here you are giving in to old jealousies.* Still he knew in his heart, in all clarity, that offering forgiveness was his only road to peace of mind. Let the rest of it go, he told himself. Depart this life with dignity. Offer forgiveness to those who have trespassed against you, and go in peace. Submit to the wisdom of the Almighty; turn the other cheek. Whatever you do, don't lose control of yourself. Doing so would ruin everything.

MARIAN

There were times when she wished Virgil would let well enough alone, and she continued to grimace in his wake. It wasn't that he was bossy so much as he liked having his way without saying so. Acting overjoyed just then and waltzing around her mother over a new account wasn't something Marian had any wish to do. What of her father, she thought as she tried to refocus on serving customers. Virgil had no idea how terrible she felt over his being sick and that she had all but shunned him all these years. As for Ron—well okay, she had to get him told, but did Virgil think she was unaware of that?

That Ron was never with her at times like these, even by phone, just reaffirmed the differences between them, Marian thought. Still, did Virgil think it was easy to say to your husband, with a flick of the wrist, hey, I'm pregnant, one, and two, I'd like you to move out, because I've had it up to here with you and I'd like a divorce? Did he think she could just open a can of worms like that and toss it in someone's face? But she did have to get Ron told and was tempted to call right then. The force was with her—to lay him out with no less cool than a movie queen in a Technicolor moment on the big screen.

She knew what Ron would say: "Hey, babe, busy right now, get back to you in a few, okay."

How could she tell anyone in the wide world that Ron's singular interest for weeks—with his buddies Petey, Greg, the Tomster—had been researching combinations of beer, legumes, restraint, and anal "embouchure." Embouchure, she had learned, was a technique for releasing sound from wind instruments such as flutes and tubas. Their goal: to compete in Toronto in November in the Book of World Records Farting Contest. "Hey babe, c'mon with us to Toronto—it'll be a toot in more ways than one." She could barely allow herself to live with him, let alone engage him in serious conversation. Bending over backwards and farting into a microphone on stage. "Whaddaya mean pregnant—I thought we were taking precautions? Whoa, babe, this isn't what I was counting on."

Marian wished for the moment that she'd gone with her father long ago and become a lobsterwoman, running a boat of her own. Freedom and independence. She'd be a local character—a few hardy women ran boats up around Camden and Vinalhaven but not here—and that was okay. She'd have time to think, and her little baby would be proud to have her as her mother. As for the Thomaston deal, so they had landed an account. You'd think it was exclusive rights to pasta in the North End. Prisoners making toys, bagel racks, perpetual wooden calendars. Hey, Jude, wow. The artifacts were authentic to Maine, all right, and so was the mentality that thought they were a big deal.

Oh, well, be fair, Marian told herself. Running a store may not have been something she had asked for but it was worse than ungrateful to resent what her mother had done for her. She loved her mother, her mother was her best friend, yet Marian knew she herself was more like her father—more reflective and not so gregarious or given to being popular and successful. On that thought, wrapping wine glasses in tissue paper, she pressed the last of four into a bag and felt it crack. Coming back to herself, to the customer, she said, "I'm sorry, I'm in too much of a rush—I'm sorry." She removed the glasses, confirmed that but one was broken, and went to the shelf for a replacement. She apologized again as she wrapped the new glass and repacked the bag. "Something on my pea brain," she said and the white-haired lady, smiling, said, "Honey, don't worry about it."

Standing there, gazing within, Marian saw that she did not know what she wanted from the world. She wished she could feel about the store the way her mother did. How wonderful it would be to love this space like that. To have it as a dream, and also not to feel alone with herself all the time and unable to tell others what she was thinking—or they'd think she was unappreciative, or even silly. Or, like Ron, would think she was spoiled. How nice it would be. Other people felt like that, didn't they?

Ron remained on her mind. She was imagining getting him told, speaking to him on her cell phone in a close-up moment, and, in the next instant, came to herself—the force was taking her over—really was unflipping her phone as she walked to the front door and out to the sidewalk. Nor did she hesitate as she reached the breezy air, punching the familiar digits—*punch! punch!*—as if they were Ron's nose and he had to know she was at the end of her rope. The force was with her all right; let the chips fall where they may. "Ron Slemm!" she called to be heard through motors and fans filling the air around her. She disliked his name, always had.

"He's—"

"It's his wife—it's important!"

He came on and she called, "There's something I have to tell you."

"Hey—"

"I'm going to have a baby, okay. I know that's nothing you want, but that's the way it is. And I know I don't want to live with you anymore. What I want is a divorce, as soon as possible. I want you to take your friends, your stupid farting contest, I want it out of my life—"

"What're you on—you drunk?"

"Yeah, right, I'm drunk. With a little baby in my belly, that's what I do, is get drunk. Grow up! I'll tell you what I'm doing, Ron—I'm coming to my senses! And I have to go now because I'm working. I just want you to know what the deal is because—"

"Marian, hold it a second, please, okay? You sound like you're losing it. You want to talk about things, fine, we'll talk about things. I'm sorry, whatever it is, I'm sorry, and we'll talk about it. Just cool down, okay. You're pregnant? You're kidding? You sound like you're about to blow a gasket."

"I'm not kidding. And I won't be cooling down. My father's dying, too—okay? With lung cancer. I can't live like a teenager anymore! It's making me sick of who I am!"

"Marian, let's talk about it, okay, after work? It sounds like you've been blindsided, and we'll talk about it, but not on the phone, okay? Listen, I know I haven't been real responsible lately, but I'll change, I swear. The farting thing, it's over, I'm sick of it myself. Let's talk after work, when we can sit down and be calm. I understand you're upset, I understand, and I don't blame you—"

She snapped the mouthpiece shut and cut him off. And she sighed as she glanced around the parking lot at the coming and going of cars and shoppers. Tears would have been relieving, but at the moment she had no feeling for them, not over Ron. As in high school, tears would have meant a crisis was over and they were making up—

she would have welcomed it deeply—but now there were no tears and what she knew within was that she had to hold her own. It was going to be next to impossible, but it was what she had to do. She couldn't live another day the way she had been living. There were things to be said for marrying an older man, and right now they made perfect sense. She wanted adulthood in her life. Common sense. Intelligence. Wit and humor. And she hoped she could make things right with her father when she saw him after work. Above all, she wanted to get through to him with a message of love and understanding, before he was lost to her forever.

Virgil was holding forth and the toast was proceeding as Marian, still trembling, arrived in the rear of the store. Her mother gave her an expression that said where have you been? are you holding up okay? Virgil handed her a glass and, bottle in hand, reached to fill the delicate crystal with champagne bubbles and shooting stars.

"This lady knew in her gut from day one!" Virgil said, swiveling back around, drawing laughs and smiles. "That Thomaston line was locked up—and ready to break out!" The group of ten or twelve, including some customers and other part-timers, continued to grin and snicker, and, not for the first time, Marian thought, well, maybe they have something there. The laminated woodcraft items would always provoke conversation over where they had come from, no doubt about that. Hands and hearts of stricken souls. As Virgil said, they carried stories.

Stepping over to be next in line to embrace her mother, she wondered if she didn't also need to grow up. Her mother whispered, "Honey, I love you so much," and Marian's eyes filmed yet again. Well, you don't come of age at twenty-one but at twenty-seven, was the thought crossing her mind. You get pregnant, open your eyes, and all at once you grow up. She'd have to explain it to her mother. She could see her smile, could hear her laughter bubbling up.

WARREN

Beatrice had yet to call. Deciding to let the answering machine take her reply, he left again, this time for the Co-op, to surrender his traps and fishing grounds. Giving up his grounds was a form of suicide he found hard to admit he was committing—yet it had to be done and all at once he wanted to get it behind him.

How long was "after a while"? Or had she said "half an hour," which would have elapsed more than an hour ago? If he could offer them forgiveness and extend a hand by way of saying good-bye, all that he wanted would fall into place. She knew his condition—what choice did she have but to name a time? If she felt threatened, let her bring Virgil. Think how surprised they'd be when they heard that he was offering friendship and forgiveness, was letting them off the hook.

Dragging himself out to his truck, Warren felt a degree of calm. He had decided to give his traps away with his grounds because hauling gangs of gear to process and sell separately was more than he could handle. The best scenario was to have Joe DiMambro say to a young fisherman, here, you're granted this area and the traps that are in place. Green-and-white buoys. It's what he'd like if he were on the receiving end, Warren thought. Area marked by traps in place, courtesy of Warren Hudon. No strings attached.

Grounds surrendered, he'd have Beatrice to speak to one last time and all would be in place.

Then—he didn't care. He'd lie back and watch baseball until nature had her way. Or he'd stare into space, for any comfort it might give him to think of things. Going without chemicals was how to do it, he was ever more certain. Wasn't it in fighting death that pain rose to be endured—fighting, though death always had its way in the end? Wasn't it in gazing upon the horizon that animals, in their greater wisdom, crossed to the other side? Had nature not long ago let man know how to die?

Unconsciousness might occur like the sun going down, the light of the world going out, Warren thought. Fear was passing from him, and his only concession would be to ask for morphine if physical pain became unbearable, but he hoped not to ask for anything. He'd relish any thoughts to come his way—for thinking was life, and even as he hungered for death he wanted his mind to remain clear until the end.

"I guess I've got the obituary blues, if you know what I mean," he tried to joke as he settled into a chair opposite Joe DiMambro's desk at the Co-op. He had asked for a confidential chat with the door closed, and DiMambro had moved around to close them in, even drew Warren a partial mug of coffee from a stained glass pot on a side table.

"Gee, Warren, I don't think I like the sound of that."

"Well, there you have it. Cancer's got me, and there's not much to do about it." A cough issued, as if for punctuation.

"God, Warren, that's hard to hear. I've been worried about you. We all have."

"I appreciate that," Warren said, trying to smile. "I saw the doc yesterday and he said it's terminal. Wouldn't say how much time, except not much. Don't plan any long trips, is what he said."

"Warren, good Lord."

"There's something to be said for knowing ahead of time—gives you a chance to put things in order."

"Oh, I understand, still—"

"What it is, I wanted to ask your help with some things."

"Of course, anything."

"Beatrice'll be selling my boat, I expect. Everything's going to her and she'll be coming around for help with the boat. As for my grounds and traps, I won't be running them anymore—couldn't if I wanted—and if you'll make up something for me to sign, for you to bear witness, I'm leaving it all to the Co-op. What I'd like is for the members to take up a vote either for a lottery for all of it to go to one man, under twenty years of age in any case—I'm insisting on that—or to divide the grounds between a couple each under twenty years of age. Only got a handful of traps out there right now, altogether, but they mark out the grounds. Not that much these days, but a decent stake, say, for a young man starting out." Warren paused a moment as DiMambro stared at him. "That's about it," he added. "That's what it comes to."

DiMambro seemed not to know what to say or do.

Nor did Warren; then he said, "You draw up a paper in two copies, I'll sign them right now. You keep one, I'll take one with me."

"You've thought this out, you're sure you don't want an attorney present?"

"I've thought it out."

DiMambro appeared flustered for another moment, then reached for a pad of paper and ballpoint pen.

Warren said, "If I can't trust you, what's it all amount to?"

"Warren, I'll do my best to see your wishes are carried out, just like you say. Still, I would advise having an
attorney present."

"You would, for sure?"

"I would, yes."

"Well, I guess I don't want to. He's a lawyer, you
know."

"Ah."

"Just give me your word. Like I say, I can't trust you,
as a friend, what's it all amount to?"

"Warren, I'll stand by my word."

"We're just fishermen. We're not lawyers."

"I'll stand by my word."

"Thank you, Joe, I know you will."

"Shall we write it up? I'll put it on the machine so
we can have a look at it."

DiMambro went through the steps as if it were nothing
more involved than a membership agreement, and in a
few minutes, asking questions to clarify points of land and
rock outcroppings that defined the boundaries, had a copy
clattering like Morse code from the machine's printer.

"Can we call Joe Jr. on this as a witness?" Warren
said.

"Well, he's under twenty, so there'd be a conflict
there."

"Let's just sign it then."

"I don't think there'll be any problem. The grounds are well known and all the members will know what's what."

Warren signed each copy first, then Joe DiMambro signed and came up with envelopes into which to place the separate copies.

"My father fished those grounds thirty years and I've fished them thirty myself," Warren said. "His father fished them too, you know."

DiMambro gazed at him. "That's sad in a way. But giving the grounds to a youngster. You couldn't do a finer thing than that."

Warren had little idea what else to say, nor did DiMambro and for a moment they sat in silence, two aging men not knowing quite how to look at each other with the present subject between them.

Driving home, Warren accepted, on a simple turn of mind, that the end of the road was in view. His fishing grounds were gone, and he could as well have signed away his home and been walking down the street with no place ever again to rest his head. What else was he to do? He loved his daughter and, only here, for the first time, understood the ease of transition a parent might know in having a child to whom to bequeath the reins of life. Beatrice would have that one day with Marian, he thought. It was yet another way in which she had closed him out, another trespass for which he would have to turn the other cheek, to make real his offer of forgiveness.

BEATRICE

She was cleaning her glasses with a cotton hanky, one of her gestures when beset by anxiety. She and Virgil were alone in the office, and he had one more errand to run before returning to take her to lunch. "Would you like *me* to talk to him?" he was saying.

It would only make things worse, Beatrice was thinking and she shook her head. "He's so determined about this favor—that's what's not like him."

"Well, I won't have you meeting him in a public place—whatever he means by that. I won't have that."

Beatrice had little idea what to say, to Virgil, Warren, anyone. By now she only wanted the problem to go away, and was thinking she'd grant Warren his favor if he'd just say what it was he was talking about. Anything to have it done with.

"I'll do whatever you want me to," Virgil was saying, about to leave. "I don't mind talking to him."

"That's okay. He says it's just some sentimental question."

Virgil kissed her on the cheek. "We'll celebrate at lunch, then pick up the note at the bank. That's the thing to keep in mind—you've won this account! You watch,

people are going to devour that line. It's terrible about
Warren, it really is—but let's not let it spoil what it doesn't
have anything to do with. Okay?"

On a fond look, as she nodded, Virgil was gone, and
Beatrice, standing at her desk, tried to find a way to agree
with what he had said. She needed time with Marian, she
thought, to talk over all that was going on. They should
go out for dinner, just the two of them—a late meal and
a chance to talk, because the best medicine for both of
them would be to log some solid hours at work and sort
things out. Nothing helped like logging solid hours. She
might even let Marian know that when the dust settled,
and if she wanted, she could move in with her. She could
have the baby at home, where there was space and it
would be easy to help her out. It was delicate stuff, all of
it—life and death—but it would be easier to endure if they
had some moves in mind down the road.

And she couldn't help thinking how pleasant it would
be to open up the house again. To refurbish its dark and
divisive decor, fill it with music boxes and nursery rhymes,
with sunlight and innocence. It was a sizable house, within
view and sound of the harbor, and what a relief it would
be to have it free of the dark presence that had filled it all
these years. A new lease on life—knowing freedom and
having a baby to love and spoil. A little girl with silken
hair to comb and caress—maybe a boy who would adore
his gramma. Going home each day, she'd be ripe with

joy. It wasn't something she'd admit, and it pained her to think of forsaking Warren in his time of need, but she longed for things to be settled. Yes, to be free of him. To have rooms painted new colors. Ivory and eggshell in place of those browns and tans. What she was thinking was awful, she knew, and she'd never tell a soul—at the same time, ever since she'd read his note and begun to sense he was using his condition to get back at her, that in itself reinforced her urge to be free of him. A new life, at her age, and a baby in the house! Virgil could visit, and she would cook him a big meal! Maybe happiness would be theirs after all.

She was stepping from the office when Lori let her know from the front counter—hand over receiver—that Mr. Hudon was on the line, and Beatrice took the call, ready to deal with him once and for all.

Even before she could speak, though, Warren was saying, "You said you'd let me know—it's been hours!"

"Warren, don't snap at me or I won't talk to you at all!"

"I'm not snapping. I just want to get things settled."

"That's exactly what I want."

"I'm having a bad time—please, don't be hard on me."

"I don't mean to, Warren—but I am going to be straight with you. I don't know what it is you want, this favor you're talking about. I'm sure I'd grant it if I knew what it was. But I am *not* going to meet with you in a public place. That is not going to happen. So please, tell me what it is you want, tell me now, and I'll do the best I can."

Warren, sounding like he was suppressing gravel in his throat, said, "What I want, is just for us to meet. That's the favor. I can't just say what I have to say over the phone. The favor is to meet and for you to hear what I have to say. It has to be in person."

"Well, I can see you at home tonight—though it'll have to be late because I'm taking Marian out to eat."

"We can't meet now—for ten minutes? Beatrice, I gave up my traps and fishing grounds. I'm having a hard time here. I only want to make up a bit, while I have a chance, that's all. Can't you bend a little? I just need to see you. Just ten minutes."

She paused, holding the receiver, tightening her jaw and resolve. Sensing she had to pull a difficult trigger, she said, "Warren, listen to me now. I don't mean to be unkind—I don't—but I'm not going to let you manipulate me. I'm sorry, but it's what I believe you're trying to do. I'm sorry you're sick—but I can't let you use that to make me do something I don't want to do or that I find threatening. Is that so hard to understand?"

Warren took in a breath. "I only need to see you, so I can"— he coughed—"so I can speak my mind, that's all."

"Warren, I think you're trying to get back at me. I wish I didn't, but I do."

"For God's sake, Beatrice, I'm sick."

"You could have gotten treatment," she said at last. "You said yourself you've been sick for months. Warren, I'm sorry about all of this, but what I think is happening is you're trying to drag me over the coals. I'm sorry."

"Well, maybe you're right," he said after a moment. "You're always right, aren't you?"

"Another problem is I'm scheduled for a late lunch, it would have to be another day in any case."

"Today's the only day. I don't know if I'll have other days."

"Warren, please—I can't listen to this."

"Is Virgil there?"

"He's not, but it wouldn't make any difference if he was."

"You know I can tell when you're lying."

"Well, tell what you like."

"It changes your voice."

Beatrice held silent.

"You don't have to lie," Warren said. "Not anymore. I've wondered, you know, if you have any idea how I've lived with what you've done to me all these years. Being by myself, while you were with him. Do you know how it feels to be all alone? I was your husband, and you lied to me every day, even when you didn't say anything."

His words stung. She didn't speak for a moment. And then, after all the years of looking away, her impulse was to purge it all. "You're not completely innocent yourself," she got out. "I knew, a long time ago, I knew things wouldn't work for us, and I'm sorry—but Warren, you had to know what was going on. You can't blame everything on me for how your life has gone. That may hurt, but it is the God's truth."

After a moment, Warren said, "You did know, didn't you—you knew, years ago, that we didn't stand a chance."

"Warren, I can't go on with this."

"You both knew. You knew how it had to be for me. Why didn't you leave? Why didn't you let me go?"

"For that I am sorry, that's what I'm saying."

"Well, I am, too, if you want to put it that way. That's some of what I wanted to tell you—I'm sorry for thinking, back then, that I owned you. It's what I felt, but I didn't know it was wrong. It's what I thought it was to have a wife. I didn't mean to hold you down, if that's what I did. If I could do it again, I wouldn't do that."

"Well, it's history," she said, and blinked against weeping. "There's no need to call it up."

"It's what I thought marriage was."

"Warren, please, let's just let it go."

"Did you give yourself to Virgil—like you never did to me? Is that something you can tell me?"

"Warren, I don't care to talk about any of this."

"I wish I could understand why it works for some and not for others."

"Warren, please."

"I've never asked you these things, but it would've helped if you'd told me how you felt a long time ago."

"I can't talk anymore. It's history—nothing can be done about it."

"Maybe I could have done something with my life."

Beatrice hesitated before saying, "Warren, if this is the favor you wanted, that's my answer. I can't say any more."

"What I wanted to tell you, one thing, is if you hadn't been my wife, I'd have admired you at a distance, like a lot of people do. I wanted to think you didn't give yourself to Virgil either, that it wasn't just me who was treated like that. I don't know if that's something you can tell me, but I'd like you to if you could."

"Warren, I can't talk anymore. I'm sorry. All this does is bring up sad feelings, and I have to get back to work. I've listened to you now, it's the best I can do. I'm going to hang up now."

"Is Virgil there?"

Beatrice sighed. "Warren, I told you twenty-five years ago Virgil was here." Warren did not respond, and she added, "You weren't listening then, and you're not listening now."

He still did not respond.

"Warren, I'm going to tell you something that's hard to say: I'm sorry you're sick, but I'm *not* responsible for the decisions you've made in your life. I hope you understand that. You've made your choices. Blame me if you like—I deserve some of the blame, I admit it—but you've made your own choices."

She replaced the receiver. Steeling herself, she took up papers and pen from her desk, trying to move elsewhere in her mind, trying to get her heart to settle down.

VIRGIL

He pressed the horn of his Stealth bomber and uttered under his breath, "Kindly get out of my way!" And as a mint green Tercel with out-of-state plates dragged its indecisive butt from the narrow right-of-way, Virgil squeezed by and, a hundred yards along, nosed into the lot of York Village Guaranty Trust. He hated to rush but had no choice if he was going to be back in time for his luncheon date with Beatrice.

Closing his car door—what happened to that weather they'd been having?—he made his way through the bank's rear entrance and past its ATM machines. His double life was rearing its head and disrupting his balanced eye. It was a two-step he had danced adeptly for decades, from Kittery to Augusta to York Village, from properties and accounts receivable to conferences and his quiet office

with a view. Each family knew of, and ignored, the other—
so long, really, as cash and power continued to be available—and each believed its bond to be special, one by
blood, one by affection, and neither was wrong. Nor did
Virgil mind the patriarchal quicksteps he had danced for
years, of a mind that they had kept him on his toes and
young at heart. When one or another pressed too hard or
too close he had always been able to get out of town, or
give himself to days of work in his office, studying briefs
and taking calls in the third floor space overlooking Portsmouth Harbor, occasionally passing a night or two on the
foldout couch.

Only when he was pulled both ways at once—as he
was today—did his teeth clamp down. That fool Warren,
and now the second of his two daughters waiting for him
to provide down payment and cosigning of a note—in
an enterprise he had not believed in for a second and knew
would be his to assume within two years, three at most.
Virgil both loved and disliked his two daughters, bearing
a weaker spot for this youngest of his three children (thank
God for Bruce, his oldest, away at Sherman Adams Law
School), while all concerned knew that the transaction
about to take place had more to do with blackmail than
the securing of a thirty-year note. "You have to do this
for Tessie," his wife had told him eye to eye. Tessie, mis-
chievous, undisciplined, chunky as always, had said,
"Daddy, it's your duty to give us a dowry to squander—

why do you think Robbie married me?" Tessie always made him grin and snort, if forlornly, and allow her passage into his guilty heart.

The down payment was $18,000 to secure a note of $162,500, to acquire a convenience store and attached three-bedroom home for Tessie and her acne-scarred husband of eleven months, each of whom had exhausted any visible means of income—she, recently, from part-time gift shop clerking, he as a temporary vinyl siding applicator. Robbie made super subs and they'd work all the hours themselves, Tessie had assured him. At least they have a dream they're willing to work for, Abby had added. They wouldn't even *think* of hiring part-time help until they were well on their feet, Tessie had said.

To help with what? Virgil had wanted to say, given that the previous three owners, over a seven-year period, had closed due to lack of business. And yes, the sub of Robbie's creation he had taken to his office for lunch had been wonderful—but what had been the cost of the multiple layers of hard salami, prosciutto, roast beef, and two kinds of imported cheese? Whom would they be catering to, Rockefellers taking the wrong exit from the Interstate, or local working stiffs willing to pay thirty dollars for a sandwich to gobble with their Pepsi?

"Daddy, you have to give us a chance, it's the least you can do," Tessie had said, giving him her knowing smile and tear-filled eye. Poor Tessie. Virgil knew she didn't stand a chance in life and he melted every time. No dirty little secrets where she was concerned; she was a lovable loser and a father's, and politician's, scary dream.

The mortgage officer had them waiting at a large table, and when he entered with documents and a pretty assistant, sixteen minutes late by Virgil's watch, he avoided eye contact, neglected to greet them—Tessie and Robbie were homely, there was no getting around it—and continued an anecdote he had been addressing to his young assistant about a colleague having had his car towed for illegal parking. Virgil took it as roostering for the benefit of all (women were so superior at working with the public, he couldn't help thinking) and wished he had dressed casually, even worn blue jeans, for the small power-surprise he could inflict on unsuspecting bankers and clerks. The young mortgage officer, for his part, was wearing green sailboat suspenders, having left his suit coat elsewhere, and was taking his time with his story as he separated documents into neat piles before his place at the table.

Virgil could resist it no longer and said, "Any time today."

"Sir?" the young man said.

"You didn't hear me—would you like me to write it down?"

"I beg your pardon."

"As well you should. You arrive fifteen minutes late, now you dally around and ignore our presence. Has it ever occurred to you that some of us might have other things to do?"

"Daddy, we're here to ask for a loan," Tessie stage-whispered.

"Sir, the bank gives careful attention to mortgages."

"Well, let's call the bank's president and ask his opinion of your careful attention—shall we do that?"

"Sir, you are?"

"I'm Virgil Pound, who might you be?"

A crimson flush climbed the young man's neck, and he said, "Sorry, Mr. Pound, I didn't know who you were. Very sorry to keep you waiting."

"Let's just get on with it," Virgil said.

Back on the highway, Virgil was pleased that his son-in-law had been witness to his little display of authority. It'll get him working, he thought. It won't *keep* either of them working—they were as easy to read as a comic strip—but it might scare them into heightened activity for at least a while. Soon, though—Virgil was certain—there would be reports of business not being as good as they had hoped, the cost of inventory being higher than expected, the hours being oppressive, and, surprise, of a rankling between the two of them from spending so much time together. Then, before another spring bird chirped from

a branch in the north, there would come the tearful confession from Tessie that they could not pay the mortgage,
that she was terribly unhappy, that she didn't know what
to do.

Tomorrow's heartache, Virgil told himself as he drove
along. He knew only that when the time came he'd tell
them no, they had had their chance, and his personal life,
and Mrs. Hudon's personal life, had nothing to do with
how anyone else conducted their affairs. Adulthood was
a world predicated on work and money, on earning
enough to pay one's way and to sustain one's balance of
health and happiness, which realities many young people,
to their dismay, took for granted and had no choice but
to learn the hard way, which way they themselves had
obviously chosen. When teachers warned of living to regret not doing one's work, he would tell them, this was
what they had had in mind. Nor was it going to get any
better. They could kid themselves, or they could dig in
and make the best of a bad situation. Or they could step
in front of an eighteen-wheeler on I-95. Scramble or be
splattered, he would tell Tessie and her husband. Those
were their choices.

Not that he hadn't made mistakes himself, Virgil
thought, because he had. His good fortune, though, was
that his mistakes had occurred earlier rather than later,
and there had been time to become resourceful, which
he had done while stronger boys were driving cars and

fighting over girls, all of whom—like his daughters and their husbands—would prove to be spoiled, dependent, overweight missers-of-the-boat. All through school he had been bullied by stronger boys, and attractive young women like Beatrice Scott had had nothing to do with him. But his day had come and his confidence had grown, while the confidence of many of the strong boys had atrophied by age twenty-five. In that respect Beatrice had been a godsend to him, for the heightened confidence she gave him, though she may not have known what a neophyte state representative he had been when she first came into his life. To think of the terror he had known as a schoolboy when older boys had pushed him around. No dirty little potency for him in those affairs of give-and-take, for they were all give. It was a time in his life he would never reveal to Beatrice, in awareness that it could only diminish him in her penetrating eyes. She who was a creature more gifted than she herself might ever know. It might stimulate him to know her husband was locked outside the bedroom door, but he wouldn't gain her vote in telling her so.

BEATRICE

She had not told Warren off but had come close enough to feel some satisfaction. She had declared, as she had long wanted to, that Virgil was the man in her life. Her words may have been unkind, given his condition, but at least they were true. There had been another time, early in their marriage, when she had tried to have him know what was true and he had refused to hear her then, too. Her mistake—her cowardice, she had always believed—was that she had failed to say outright that she was enamored of the Maine State Representative from the Thirty-sixth District, that though both were married and he had three small children, they were together every day, at meetings, lunches, in cars and on walks, that they had fallen in love and there were ever more crossings of the line, by him, by her, touches, looks, caresses, small kisses that had grown enchanting—a flowering intimacy she wouldn't risk violating by attempting to explain, but which, she imagined, only a blind man could fail to see.

Warren's perception had remained dim, however, and she still blamed herself for not having been more clear, notwithstanding Virgil urging her at the time not to rock the boat. The initial storm came to a head on a Sunday afternoon when they were at a cookout at her family's place in Portsmouth, though Warren's mother and an uncle from Casco Bay were also there. The time to leave had arrived and Warren, young and more strapping than he would ever be again, had carried Marian, asleep in the baby carriage basket they used as a car crib, placed her in the backseat of the car, and returned to where Beatrice remained in conversation, caught up in talk having to do with her job, with excitements of life long since forgotten. Warren told her a second and third time to come on, the baby was in the car, and she raised a hand to say just a minute, to please let her finish what she was saying.

She had followed Warren's lead in those days despite her growing infatuation for her boss. It had yet to become an affair—which word alone terrified her. At the same time she was also growing infatuated with her work, where deeper responsibility, small doses of authority, and even political leverage had begun to intoxicate her just as they intoxicated Virgil Pound of York Harbor. Still, she had taken into marriage a belief of women deferring to men, as had Warren, though she had begun—a certain embarrassment to them both, as her boss was not ungenerous with salary increases—to easily outearn her husband in his scrabbling enterprise as an independent lobsterman.

And, deep into that backyard cookout conversation, she once again raised a hand to him when he said "Beatrice!" and added, she would always remember, "Just a minute, Warren!" and wasn't really irritated, nor was he when he said something of her becoming a state legislator herself, to the amusement of all.

It was then that it happened, and while everyone laughed, her relatives included, and though several men applauded as if they were townsfolk in a movie starring Gary Cooper, the helplessness and humiliation, the anger she felt would change her life forever, and Warren's too, though neither had a clue of that at the time.

Warren picked her up—physically—wrapped his arms around her waist and legs and carried her like a squirming child.

She had been making a point about something and all at once he lifted her away. She had always been a small woman, hardly broke a hundred pounds in those days, but wasn't a child, of course, nor was her life part of a silly movie in which men won the West while women cooked and cleaned, and, going into shock as he carried her off, had madly ordered him to put her down, immediately.

He ignored her demands and went on, though her anger had her in tears and thrashing so wildly it became an embarrassment to all.

They reached the car in the driveway before he placed her on her feet. She half-froze, her situation impossible in every way. She could not return to the cookout and instruct them to think differently—if they needed to be so instructed—nor could she enter the car with any measure of self-respect yet in place. *"How dare you—don't you ever touch me like that again!"* she said, and her outrage was such that the impulse rising in her was to fight back with such ferocity that she would injure him physically for what he had done to her.

She entered the car in silence. He made sounds of apology, then and later, but no matter, the damage had been done and, in her heart, their marriage came to an end during the harsh moments of silence on the drive home. She sat there knowing he had given her the opportunity to sever herself from him once and for all, and so she would. In the car and in the moments of returning their sleeping infant to her railinged bed, her heart called to Virgil, and she decided to seize life as it was there to be seized, to forgo husband and marriage no matter the consequences, to convey to Virgil, tomorrow, that she was ready to enter into supreme intimacy with him, that she wanted his love in the way that love from a powerful man might give her the strength she needed to realize the person she believed in her heart she was destined to be. She might be breaking her vows in some eyes while in her own mind she was being true to herself. She might live a lie, as a woman, but would do so with independence and courage.

She told Warren that the gap between them was irreparable, but, on Virgil's advice, did not break from him, which may have been her crucial mistake. Virgil had cautioned against making themselves vulnerable—said his political life and all else would be up for grabs, as would her custody of her precious child, if the love they knew for each other should become known.

Warren came apologizing every day, and she turned a deaf ear. A week, ten days passed, during which time she refused to speak to him, took comfort in her work, her child, and found fulfillment beyond her wildest dreams in a motel room, a locked office, in the rear seat of a state limousine with shaded windows, went fully into a relationship of passion and heightened political power, of glorious consummation. She became a true woman, and love and passion of an exalted kind rose into place within her breast and mind. She had never felt so alive and, in her impassioned state, did not care what Warren did or said, or if he lived or died.

He came apologizing still, trying to joke, to understand, begged forgiveness and begged at last that she at least speak that they might proceed through meals, daycare needs, paying of bills, and shopping with minimum confusion and duplication. She spoke, agreed to speak to that degree. He smiled some, and his eyes glossed up as if the war had ended and she would love him still, or again, though she assured him her speaking was only for the convenience of daily life. Privately, she disdained the tail-between-the-legs puppy-dog love she knew he retained for her and welcomed the power over him her curious victory had gained her. She also vowed in her heart to give herself ever more deeply to the man she loved, to further nurture and bolster him as he was nurturing and bolstering her.

Hardly a week passed before Warren confronted her again, demanding an account of what was happening,

and it was then that she tried to give it to him straight—
but for the illicit love which was making her strong. "You
took me for granted, treated me as a doormat, and I can't
forgive you for that," she told him. "You assumed you
would lead in all ways, and I would follow, and my
earning power is already nearly double yours. You
treated me like that in front of my family, and the humiliation was an assault on my person I will never get
over. I may not think of it every day, but you should
believe me when I tell you I will never get over it, not
as long as I live."

She reduced him to tears. He tried not to cry, but
was unable to help himself. He said he had done it only
as a joke, like something in a movie. He said he'd had
several beers, in case she had forgotten, was feeling frisky,
in fact. Far from wanting to humiliate her, he had wanted
to have her in his arms, to love her. He hadn't meant to
humiliate her. Could she never forgive him?

She paused, and decided to wield the blow she believed would gain her her freedom. "Not even if I wanted
to," she told him, and the words issued as if from a larger
power. "I hope you hear what I'm saying. Not even if I
wanted to. It's not in me to be anyone's possession."

He did not hear, however, and confronted her another
time, though when he'd been drinking, asking if she no
longer wanted him in any way as a husband—and she

spoke the truth then, too, though he did nothing about it. She said to him: "Warren, the best favor you could do for yourself would be to walk out that door right now, sleep in your smelly boat, and see an attorney about filing for divorce. That's what I'd like you to do. I'll help with the attorney's retainer, in case you don't know about attorney's retainers. I don't want to hurt you, but I don't want to be married to you anymore either."

What she had neglected each time to mention was that she wanted him to save her the difficulty of initiating a separation, that she had given herself to another and that it was more attraction to Virgil than repulsion from him that was guiding her. What she couldn't say was that the elected official with whom she had fallen in love had yet again warned of his vulnerability should it come out that he was having an affair with a married or even a divorced aide. A scandal would destroy him and, ultimately, would destroy them both.

Warren took no steps to change his life and time slipped by. He fished most days, leaving before daylight, picked up Marian after school when it was raining, and fixed evening meals, while Beatrice worked late, then spent a night away for the first time, in Augusta, began spending added nights away now and then, and more than a few people in Maine and occasionally in New York, Boston,

Washington assumed—as they almost did themselves—
that they were state representative, then state senator, and
his wife, Virgil and Beatrice Pound of the Thirty-sixth
District of New England's rugged Pine Tree State.

At the same time, her love for Warren did not die entirely,
no matter her words and actions. There came another
summer evening, when she and Virgil were on a pleasure craft in Portsmouth Harbor with a party of ten or so
from out of state, and the guests were waxing sentimental over the integrity of Maine lobstermen, and for a moment she was stricken with guilt and her heart went out
to Warren—he whose life had only slid more deeply into
failure as the years had gone by. Virgil, drinking, had made
an unkind aside to her, near the railing there in the twilight. "Hope we don't see a boat with Cuckold on the
back," he tittered, stepping to the bar for a refill, and
Beatrice could not help recalling Warren taking her to
Narrow Cove in high school to show her *Lady Bee*
painted along the bow of his Jonesporter, and, finding
herself stricken with guilt there among Virgil's guests,
could not help breaking and trying to conceal the emotion overtaking her, was unable to restrain, unable even as
she leaned toward the water, and as Virgil tried to con-
sole her, told him she'd thought of something, it was okay,
she'd thought of something that had made her feel terri-

bly sad. She drank too much then herself, and strove to push her guilt as far away as boats disappearing among lights and music rippling from shore.

WARREN

It came to him like a missing piece of a puzzle that she had known all along they did not stand a chance as husband and wife. He couldn't get over it. Why hadn't she done something about it? If she and Virgil loved each other, why had they remained apart? Wasn't that what divorce was for—despite the Church, or even Virgil's wife and children? Had he made his own choices, as Beatrice had said? He couldn't see that he had, believed he was the one who had been manipulated—just as he was being manipulated here again.

What was she trying to do to him?

Driving to the store, coughing suppressed for the moment, taking in minnow breaths, the knowledge kept rising within Warren. His gear and fishing grounds were gone, and his capacity to breathe was slipping away. As for getting through to Beatrice—she might as well be on the other side of soundproof glass, so little of what he said seemed to reach her. He had come around to believing they could gain accord, if only in a modest way, but given her words on the phone even that small dream appeared headed for the rocks. She had known all along? Dear God, why live her whole life like that?

Still, he wouldn't give up. He would offer forgiveness and extend a hand. However ailing and confused he was, he knew that as soon as he gave in to despair any chance he had would come to an end and life's only possible meaning would escape him. And he could make his case in minutes—if he weren't beset by coughing. From lunch and half an hour, he was down to minutes in a parking lot. A few words, a look in her eye, maybe the touch of her hand. He held to a sliver of hope that she would hear him out and, alas, would relent and say, "Good luck, Warren, may the next life be better for both of us."

He could die then in peace. He would close himself into his room and not bother her again. Nature might have its way while he communed with squirrels digging out ground balls and showing the way into heaven. Leaves and soil. The living sea and time everlasting. A credit at long last for having paid his dues on earth.

The harbor came into view as Warren traced Kittery Point in his truck, and a moment from the past came to mind. He was fishing. In the boat, fishing alongside his father—when he wasn't playing baseball and dreaming he might have the whiplash swing and hawk's eye of Ted Williams, another player from a coastal city given to fishing. It was a summer evening and he tied alongside his father's boat in Narrow Cove to off-load baitfish for the next morning and to take on crates of lobsters to deliver to H. Celeste's, the distributor to Boston in those days before they had the Co-op.

Gazing into the past he could as well have been a teenager driving the outboard once more into the harbor marked all around by lamps, lanterns, bobbing inboard taillights, the sun beneath the horizon and the sky ashen, sailboats and yachts with golden cabin lights like a luxury hotel extending bracelet fashion over the water. Gentle music from the tall white boats rode the waves put up by muffled propeller traffic coming and going, and, catching a sign from two men in dark jackets and white trousers on the fantail of a fifty-foot alabaster yacht, he cut his motor and puttered alongside to carry out business within reach but not within touch of the pleasure craft and its aromas of tobacco and whiskey, privilege and mysterious ways.

"Would you have a dozen you could sell?" the man called down, and Warren saw that it was not a second man in double-breasted blazer and flannels aboard the yacht but a boy close to his own age.

"I'll need a basket, and what size?" he called back.

"Pound-and-a-halfers is what we'd like," the man returned.

Cardboard box received, motor treading bubbles, Warren raised the lid on one of the crates and used his flashlight to highlight plugged lobsters. Selecting a dozen

—giving good weight, as instructed by his father—he used both hands to present the heavy drumming box.

"What's the going rate these days?" the man called down and, whatever it was at the time, Warren called back the amount and added, "They're twenty pounds there."

Waiting for the money to be passed down, bobbing and holding a hand to the yacht, he overheard the boy say, "You don't know they're twenty pounds, Dad—he doesn't have a scale."

"What is it you're saying—you think he'd cheat us?"

"He doesn't have a scale is all I'm saying."

"Let me tell you something, son. There comes a day you can't trust a Maine lobsterman, we're going to be in a hell of a fix in this world. These people are a rare breed. They wouldn't be cheating you, not in a thousand years."

A rare breed. Words and music had lingered as Warren pressed the accelerator and furrowed away. And the memory misted his eyes here as he drove, as he recalled his father, with whom he hadn't communed in months. His strong father had faced death in time as he was facing it now, and if there were any reunions in the next world, he'd soon be finding out. A rare breed. At least he had that same air of good intent in his pocket.

Warren stifled a cough climbing from his pickup, then paused, holding the door, to allow his throat to resettle. Raising into focus an apology from himself and reconciliation from her, he started across the parking lot toward Maine Authentic. This was it; he could wait no longer.

"Warren, I see your wife's place made the *Globe* the other day," a man called in passing and Warren could neither place the man nor absorb what it was he meant to say. The globe?

As he walked, Warren's confused mind was trying to apologize to Beatrice for his assumption of ownership—if he hadn't already done so, at least with the genuineness he was feeling now. For it was true that as a teenager he had assumed she belonged to him like a glossy new car one acquires from a lot, an object with fascinating gadgets, a convertible top, a curvaceous body to polish and parade among other first-time car owners. It was also true that she alone among the young wives of their acquaintance came to regard herself as a creature perhaps to be raced and bred, and maybe paraded, but never *owned,* and he wanted to apologize to her in those terms, too. It had hurt him always, and did still, that she withheld herself from him when he desired her so, withheld being his girl and wife in all that it meant, that his attempts to love her had done little more than force her further away and perhaps open her to the advances of another.

Had she given herself to Virgil in passionate ways she had refused even in the beginning to give herself to him? Had Virgil had the better sense to let her ride at his side in the guise of friendship? In a deep vein of admiration for her, Warren hoped she was a creature never possessed, no matter anyone's money or position or her desire to get ahead or make a name for herself. Dear Beatrice; he still wanted to love her, wanted to have her in his dreams, if only she would let him do so.

"Dad—what are you doing?"

It was Marian, coming between merchandise racks as he entered the store, and returning to himself, hoping not to give in to coughing, Warren paused, exhaled, "Sweetheart, hullo—here for a word with your mother is all. You doing okay? Happy to be having a baby? That's what I wanted to ask you."

"Oh, Dad, it isn't me I'm worried about. Did you tell your doctor to add me to your file?"

"Honey, let me talk to your mother for a minute. I'll do that, soon as I can."

Warren saw that Marian was upset, and moved along, wanting to get his business taken care of before something went wrong. He was dressed and shaved, he shouldn't be an embarrassment to them.

"Dad, I'm not sure she's in her office, let me buzz her," Marian said behind him.

"Just need to say something before this coughing starts up," he said, and there was Beatrice, before he'd taken half a dozen steps.

"Warren, what are you doing here—what do you want?"

"A minute of your time, like I said—I won't bother you again."

She closed another step, spoke pointedly, softly. "I told you on the phone, I'm busy. I'm sorry you're sick but I can't have you coming in here like this—how else can I say that?"

"Step outside with me for one minute."

"Warren, I'm not stepping anywhere, I told you that. You have something to say, say it now and leave. I just won't have this."

"Just one minute of your time."

"Warren, I'll talk to you tonight, like I said. Please don't make me call security."

"You can't give me one minute of your time?"

"You heard what I said."

"You knew all along, didn't you?"

"Warren, if you don't leave, right now, I'm calling security."

Somehow, as he coughed and raised his hand to his mouth, as he glimpsed Marian looking at him, he withdrew, though he seemed to be doing so in a dream world. His offer was hopeless. She wasn't going to take in his words, wasn't going to shake his hand, no matter what. How could he have thought she would ever give an inch?

* * *

Warren once more saw himself on the harbor of sprinkled lights in his father's outboard, but the time was forever and he was no longer of this world—as he returned to himself sitting in his pickup in the mall parking lot. Hopelessness was all he seemed to know. There was the everyday activity of pulling traps and coming up empty, the everyday futility of coming and going from house and boat and back again, of not being able to touch her silk-covered limbs and figure. Here at the end, futility was all his life had come to. Empty-handed and alone, coming and going.

MARIAN

Her mind wasn't on work but on herself, and on her mother and father and all that had gone wrong in their lives. She was cashiering purchases, handling credit cards, wrapping glass and stoneware items in tissue and placing them in bags all the while she was struggling in her mind to not be in the past with her parents, or in the present with Ron, but in the future with her baby who, in dreams she kept trying to create, was always a girl, al-

and they were together in a park near the water, a mother and her baby in a world beyond this sea of cares, and she could see the bond that defined them: Their love was pure—and the purity in her dream was giving her insight into her mother's love for her as a child and as an only daughter. Someone for whom to exist. As for her father and a father's love, they swirled beyond reach.

A customer—a young woman—remarked on the Exeter Ceramic wind chime being something she had been looking for for months, and something in the woman's smile had Marian glimpsing an answer, a balance in life after which her mother had striven all these years, one of peacefulness, confidence, fulfillment. Why did there have to be these problems in just existing, just getting along? Was there a pathway she might take for herself and her baby that would let them avoid the grief that seemed always to make life difficult and painful?

The young woman smiled as she accepted the bag with its MA logo and Marian imagined a communication in their glances, saying they understood the minefield women had to traverse each step of the way if balance were to be achieved. Understanding in a glance.

In the park, in her baby dream, Marian guided the carriage close to the water where she lifted her precious child into her arms and sat with her on a bench, looked into her eyes and saw them as one with her own. They were one in mind, as she knew she had been with her mother, and her father, too, for a time, though it had taken years for the realization to come home to her. She was looking forward to telling her mother of her new attitude about the Thomaston account. Her mother would laugh when she heard that her daughter had seen the light, and it would be laughter they would share, laced with the love Marian was experiencing in anticipation. Look who's becoming a mom, her mother would say, and they'd joke about certain daughters needing twenty-seven years to see what it was all about, and a certain someone's baby not taking her *out* of the store but bringing her *in!*

Why did her father remain beyond reach? Had she closed him out in such a way, long ago, that it was impossible for either of them to return to the other? Had she tried hard enough over the phone?

She buzzed her mother and spoke under her breath. "Mom, that was awful," she said.

"I know it was, I'm sorry."

"Is there anything we can do?"

"Honey, I don't know, I wish I did. I just can't have him coming in here like that. It's like he's spilling something. I'm sorry, but that's what it's like, and I can't let him do it. This store means so much to me. It's my child— it's like it's you, you know, and I'm sorry he's sick but I can't let him do that. Do you see how I feel?"

WARREN

Sitting in the parking lot, he had yet to turn the key and start his truck's motor. He did not know what to do or where to go and sat inhaling, exhaling, trying to return to a track from which he felt derailed. He knew he was losing threads in his mind, but had no sense of how to reconnect or regain purpose. He coughed and the cancer in his lungs felt like a hamper of damp laundry—raised pain in his chest and throat, his lungs tended toward collapsing before managing once more to expand; his eyes watered as he drew in air. He did not want to succumb here but at least he wasn't drugged with chemicals, tubes, hallucinations. At least he was thinking—wasn't that what he was doing?

When she went to Marian's room to sleep, long ago—had she known then, too? he wondered. Was it his carrying her under his arm, or had the carrying allowed her to know what she had already known? All those years Virgil had to have known, too, and they had never told him he did not stand a chance. They let him waste his life. There had been Helen at the diner and maybe she would have opened her heart to him. His wife and that slippery squid with all those tentacles, the two of them had cheated him out of his life. Wouldn't he have found something else if they had told him he didn't stand a chance? Might he be healthy today, if he hadn't been bound up so long?

Whatever his anger and self-disgust, Warren could not help continuing to love her. That was the joke of it— being stretched like a dog on a leash, straining to touch the one who had hurt him the most.

* * *

Marian had to have known, too, Warren thought. When she graduated from high school, when she married, when she telephoned yesterday with the news of her baby, she had to have known. They had all known, and had let him make a fool of himself.

He might be a topliner today with another wife and family, perhaps a strong stepson or stepdaughter after whom he would have long ago renamed the *Lady Bee*. And he might not be courting favors from angels this autumn day, but treated and cured, lending a hand to the passing on of his fishing grounds to a revered young man or young woman, working as first mate himself until the new captain had a refurbished boat in hand. That was the way to move through life. Bow out with peace of mind, and a youngster thinking of you now and then.

It was as Warren sat trying to grasp loose threads in his mind that he realized the killer whale was rolling into the parking lot before him. He stared motionlessly, as if seeing one of the large animals breach close to his boat on a calm sea, unaware it was being observed. The creature turned into a space and stopped, and it was then that ꟷꟷꟷꟷ ꟷꟷ ꟷꟷꟷ the front of his mind what seemed to have been lurking in its shadows: a desire to take his weapon in hand and resolve the ache in his heart once and for all. On a closing of his eyes he saw that it was imperative, saw through a blur that it was what he had to do. He was terrified at once, while his heart was crazed with logic and purpose. She did not want him in her store; they had known all along; they had let him make a fool of himself. Looking up, he saw Virgil slam the car door, he in his dark suit, tie, dark shoes, saw him walk toward the glass doors through which, moments earlier, he had been told to leave. "Dear God," Warren uttered, knowing he was beyond turning back, was going to burn in hell if need be.

Hands trembling, he opened the glove box and gripped the weight of the pistol in its oily bag. His heart was pounding and his eyes remained glossy as he let the Colt Python slide into his lap. He rested his forehead against the steering wheel, paused and tried to think rationally, tried to call up his evidence. Was it wrong to possess your wife in marriage? Wasn't it what marriage was, a merging as one? Hadn't it been life's purpose down through all time?

Six cartridges, each a deadly force—assuming they would work after years of lying untouched in the pilot-house lockbox. His eyes glossed over as he worked open the age-browned box and through a blur saw brass casings dotted red where the firing pin would strike. He thumbed rounds into chambers with trembling fingers, returned the cylinder home, pushed back the safety.

Slipping from truck to tarmac, he walked toward the glass doors, right arm hanging at his side, weapon near his thigh. His breathing was labored. His heart remained alive and high with conviction and excitement. She had known, they had known all along that he was wasting his time. Why hadn't they let him go?

A woman gasped, half-screamed, surprising him. Exiting as he was entering, she jerked a hand to her mouth, her eyes widened and her gasp and scream came as if from a startled child. He moved past her into the store, looking for Beatrice, mainly for Beatrice, only for Beatrice. In this encounter he would have his way with her. Logic and righteousness were on his side; he would have his way with her at last.

MARIAN

Hearing a segment of a stifled scream, she believed it was outdoors and continued working. She was scratching "Sale Item" with a red marker on tags with strings—a knotlike hair in need of a comb—and her heart was too burdened with threats and danger to be open to more. Maybe the sound had come from the radio of a teenage car, kids sashaying past with a boom box. Later she would look back and see that the sound was swallowed terror muffled by the front door. Still she had a sixth sense of people entering, and looking up saw her father for the second time within half an hour, saw he had something in his hand and knew in an instant that something unspeakable was upon them. Her mother and Virgil were in the office.

What should she do? She *knew* it was a gun in her father's hand—*knew* in her store sense, and in her family sense, that something too horrible to believe was taking place.

Yes, a gun, dear God. She tried once more to verify the object at her father's side. The world as she had known it was seizing up. "Dad, don't, don't," she heard herself cry as she moved around the counter in his direction, aware at the same time of life beneath her hand. "Please, Dad, don't do anything, my God."

He continued as if not hearing her. A woman cried out, "That man has a gun! Right there!"

Marian kept walking, then she called, screamed in an attempt—so she would later believe—to warn her mother. She was caught between rushing back to the intercom to buzz the office and running to intercept her father; what she did, suddenly, was dash back, grab the intercom—knowing it was too late, knowing there was no escape—and bawl helplessly, "Mother, it's Dad, he has a gun!" and wail at Lori, "Get the police, get out of here! Everyone, get out of here! Oh God!"

She thought to hit the alarm, to alert security, and, in a panic, returned yet again around the counter in the direction of helping her mother and father, of trying to stop whatever might be going to happen. She wanted to escape with the confused customers rushing for the door and inform arriving guards that the man had a gun, was her father, was wearing a pale green shirt, was six two, had been, had weighed one hundred ninety pounds, was frail, looked awful, maybe he weighed a hundred and twenty pounds.

But she did not run away. Instinct, heart, fear, something directed her to her parents, as if she alone possessed voice and words that might undo what was happening. Mere seconds had passed since her father had walked by with the gun, and what Marian saw next looked like a freeze-frame wavering on the VCR. Inside the office beyond her father's shoulder was her mother, staring wide-eyed at the weapon, Virgil behind her, to the side, saying something. "Dad, don't do it, please!" Marian cried, and she took added steps as if toward something that, even as it might explode, pulled her on.

Her father was talking, her mother was talking, and Virgil all at once came bolting for the door, and her father's arm jerked and a pistol shot split the air and ripped through shelves, sent glass, metal, wood splintering as Virgil, wide-eyed, ran from the office and would have knocked into her had she not pulled aside. He seemed to have been hit but kept going—in the wrong direction, Marian's store sense was telling her—toward that added part of the store where doors were unavailable and there was no escape, where customers were squatting near counters and shelves, trying, wide-eyed, to scamper and duck-walk to front or rear and safety.

Marian wailed, nearly fainted into herself, one hand to her belly, hearing her mother crying and saying she knew, yes, she knew what he was saying, certainly she understood, whereupon another shot sounded, striking her mother, slamming her in the chest, making her collapse like a rubber toy losing air, followed by words and another shot, by more sinking and her own wailing. Her father came walking, still appearing to fail to register who she was, passed her by, coughing, calling out, "Virgil! Virgil!"

Marian fell to her mother, whose lovely jacket and blouse were wet with blood, whose life was flowing from her. Marian tried to contain her mother in her arms, tried, sobbing, "Oh Mother, oh God," to contain her life within her hands. She hugged and rocked her mother as she had been rocked in childhood, bawled as she had bawled when her kitten had died, when a boy had canceled her from his life, bawled as the weight of this one person she had ever loved so unequivocally sank, gasping for air, into her arms, sank beyond any sense of appearing unladylike, mouth open, glasses hanging cockeyed from her hair, beyond any sense of soiling her clothes or staining the polished oak of her precious store. Marian rocked and wailed, tried to keep her mother's life from seeping away, pulled the rumpled weight of her closer and tighter into her arms, vowed to do anything, to make any sacrifice to have undone this awful event unfolding there in her hands.

BEATRICE

She was certain she had heard something of a scream. Danger had been in the air all morning and her heart had been on edge and on guard. She directed her ears to take in evidence—had no wish to cry wolf, women today did not cry wolf—and remained certain she had heard something in or around her store, all the while Virgil continued talking, laughing, making some point. She detected a cry—was it a cry?—thought of Marian, knew something was wrong, raised a hand to silence Virgil. "Listen!" Her eyes and ears were cocked.

Virgil angled his face in perplexity. Listened. Listened.

Something was in the store, near Marian, the front, near the cash registers; Beatrice knew something had entered the store and was approaching, knew more than she wanted to know. As she stepped over to open the door further, Marian's voice cried through the intercom, "Mother, it's Dad, he has a gun!" and Beatrice knew in a heartbeat that all she had ever worked for was falling toward the floor like a vase of flowers.

Her eyes shot to Virgil while her heart was cascading. They knew in their interwoven hearts that horrible retribution was upon them. Warren with a gun. She had always known it could happen, had known every day, had waited for it in her tortured heart and here it was but a moment away and closing upon her.

The office door was pushed fully open and there were his eyes, his withered face, his shrunken self—the weapon's steel barrel. Virgil did not move from the side of the office where he stood. "Warren, good God, let's be reasonable here," he uttered, and Beatrice knew from his voice that all was hopeless and lost.

Warren had eyes only for her eyes. He was saying something, but what it was, and what she was saying, hearing, thinking were hardly ordinary within her drumbeat of impending hurt, unfinished business, dreams unfulfilled, her store suffering violation beyond belief. More than once she heard, "Both of you, you always knew!"

She tried to process, calculate. What moves or words might save her? What appeal might get through to him in the face of no time remaining? There were his fierce eyes, the threat of him, his gun and voice, his awful authority. Was there an opening left? she was asking herself as she heard him say he had only wanted to forgive her, had only wanted to shake her hand! "You wouldn't give me one minute of your time!"

She tried to say she knew he had a complaint, of course she knew that, and there was a *crack!* and her sudden flinch as Virgil broke for the door, dashed off among candle holders, salad bowls, wind chimes, leaving her where escape was blocked and she remained the object of Warren's terrible wrath.

Reason . . . granting him his due . . . honesty, how might she get through to this person she had controlled so easily? Well, yes, she would have him know, fine, yes, of course he had the power now, it was in his hands . . . and she was certainly willing to sit down and hear him out, to give him minutes in whatever cafe or diner he'd like to visit. She would speak the truth, too, would *love* to speak the truth, because she had been its captive, too, in case it was something he had never paused to realize! Did he think it was easy being in love with a married man who was a power broker? was in demand? was attractive to other women, who went home to another? Why hadn't *he* known? Why had *he* been so incapable of being a man and doing something for himself? Why had *he* been so blind he couldn't see that he had to remain in the picture or the picture would look wrong!

"I only wanted to love you as your husband!" she heard him wail at her, as if from a distance.

Appeals kept racing through her mind: She would have him know how long and hard she had worked, how everything was falling into place at last, how they finally had the Thomaston account and she was finally going to be a grandmother—Warren, we're going to be grandparents!—to please put the gun down, to please find it in his heart to forgive her because he would ruin Marian's life, too, did he think life for her or their grandchild would ever be the same if he did what he was threatening to do? Nor had *he* been so easy to control himself—you weren't, Warren, she would have him know, coquettishly, oh so fairly—and he should know, too, that there had been a time on the harbor after dark when Virgil had laughed and said he hoped her husband hadn't named his boat *Cuckold,* and she had laughed too, she had, but then had cried and her heart had broken with horrible guilt when she saw how cruel she had been, and she was begging him, dear God, to please not hurt her, please, she was—but it was then that Beatrice tucked her chin in anticipation and was slammed in the chest, jabbed through with a hot poker, jabbed maybe again, found herself sitting down onto the floor while pins-and-needles raced throughout and dizziness traveled to her face, skull, arms.

She knew Marian was crying, knew that her beloved child was squeezing her and crying to her, knew she was doomed and sought forgiveness, sought harmony while part of her was sailing toward California, while she glimpsed a sunlit haze in the air and a roomful of giddy young women with cups and saucers, while on an autumn day a sixth-grade boy was trying to kiss her within the air of the lyric of a lovely song. She heard Marian crying, and she reached a finger to her tiny granddaughter in her white dress, sought the baby's tiny fingers and dark eyes through light on the horizon, sought its silken hair, its delicate forehead and blue veins encircling all.

VIRGIL

After lunch one day in elementary school he glimpsed a
fold of green-beige money move from a classmate's hand
into a jacket pocket on a hook, and a moment later paused
and slapped his thighs as if forgetting something and
turned back to where he could slip his fingers in upon
the fold of bills and fold them into his hand. He had seen
no one but then heard something, though only as he
turned on his way to the classroom did there come from
behind the squawky voice of Vera Burton: "I said I saw
you, Virgil! I saw what you did!"

He ignored her, moved on, avoided eye contact,
though later, under threat, saw that he would have done
better to return the money in her presence, to have made
a face at her or even offered to share it with her. (She had
premature breasts; who knew how things might have
gone?) He angled to his seat, heard her squawk again, and
hissed over his shoulder: *"Shut up!"*

He denied all. The teacher made him empty the
money and everything else from his pockets, and heard
from Leon Plourde, recovering his jacket, that his money
was missing, and, from Vera Burton, her eyewitness account, still he denied all. The money was his, they could
ask his mother, and not only that, he said, but during recess
he had heard them planning to trick him, and no, it wasn't
a lie! they were the ones lying! you could ask his mother,
you could!

In the vice principal's office, he held to his story all over again. They were instructed, one at a time, to tell their stories, and he held to his, said they were the ones lying and how could he not interrupt when they were telling lies? They could ask his mother, because it was money he was saving for a present for his dad and carried with him always, was money he was saving and shouldn't have let them see in the first place, he knew he was guilty of that, of showing off, but he could prove it was his because you could see pencil marks he had put on the border of each bill—only they were hard to see now because he had done it two weeks ago when he first started saving the money—but how could he have done that if what they said was true?!

That he had a way with words may have been lost on him at the time but awareness leaped ahead when the vice principal said at last that if Virgil wasn't willing to confess, there was nothing to be done about it, and the first rule, in any case, as every pupil knew, was not, *under any* circumstances, to leave valuables in the hallway where they could come up missing! or to show off with money! he added on a glance at Virgil. It should be a lesson to them all, he said, and they were to return to their room because the incident was over and he did not wish to hear another word about it, then or ever again!

Only years later did Virgil see that his best opportunity in crisis management may have eluded him in failing to compromise Vera at the outset when she caught him red-handed, and that an added missed opportunity, when they came from the vice principal's office and in response to Leon crying and slugging him in the back, was not to call the small boy chicken (which he knew himself to be) but to have said okay, take the money, it's yours, what do I care? nor to say he didn't fear Leon's brother at all, not for a second, though everyone knew—something he had also failed to factor into his reply—that Ronnie Plourde, an eighth-grader with facial hair, was a hockey player known for penalties, a muscle-bound boy who put the fear of God into eighth-graders, ninth-graders, teachers and coaches, too.

Still another opportunity eluded him when Ronnie Plourde called him at home and told him to bring his brother's seven dollars and three more to school the next day or he was going to smash his face like a pumpkin. Given the chance to buy his way out of a corner—not an unreasonable amount for someone caught red-handed—he chose yet again to deny, swore he did not take the money! Leon was a liar! went on trying to persuade himself that the hours of possession had made the money his and only an idiot would surrender such an enormous amount.

Off the phone, however, and as terror began taking him over, he started to pay a different price, and while he did not forgo his resolve (the money was his!) he progressed

enough in cunning that he at least considered cutting his
losses with a return call and counteroffer of $8 or $9, even
the $10 Ronnie Plourde had demanded, anything to be free
of the terror he was suffering. Only later did he see that
the countermove would have saved him the plum-sized
eyes, the bruises and taunts, the added terror with which
he lived, plus a net payment of $13, before the ordeal turned
toward concluding (he lived with it yet today). Rather, he
spent a night so frightened he hardly slept, and a day at
school so terrified he trembled at every turn, only to wet
his pants on the spot when he thought the day was over,
when, returned to his own neighborhood, believing he was
home free, pivoting to look behind him, he turned forward
again to see Ronnie Plourde step from behind a tree before him, felt shocked urine soil his pants and pride, was
pounded onto the sidewalk, pounded in the face, cried to
no avail, and had his manhood disrupted for the rest of
his life.

Such was Virgil's confused state as he crouched beside a
sliding cabinet door in the dead end corner of the store,
several aisles from Beatrice's office, that he was hoping
Ronnie Plourde and Warren Hudon would both die once
and for all and leave him alone. His arm was bleeding
but the wound—ripped near his armpit as if by a nail—
was not life-threatening, and what kept racing through his
mind was how feeble he had sounded when the chips

had been down ("Can't we be reasonable here!"), that he had left Beatrice to her fate with her insane husband, that after thirty years of offering to care for her, to support her in all ways and run interference for her, he had been the one to run (what else was he to do?!) and might be seen to have acted unmanly.

It happened so fast—he imagined explaining. There was no opening, he had to run for help, was a miracle the shot he received wasn't worse . . . just inches . . . and it was then that he heard Warren's cough and his voice calling his name, then that he collapsed within in recognition of his own mortality.

Still, generating some grit, he duck-walked past an aisle, crouched ever more compactly, face and wet cheek nearly to the floor, gasping, to see if he might yet escape through the main door, or (as he imagined telling reporters) to see if it were possible to disarm Warren by jumping him from behind. He pressed to a cabinet, bleeding down his right side, damp with blood in his armpit, praying his chance was real, when footsteps, shoes, khaki pant legs and the disgusting cough entered the aisle, approaching, brown shoes belonging, he knew, to Warren Hudon, he with whose wife he had carried on a lifelong affair, whose person he had vilified a thousand times or more, he whose hand carried that unanswerable weapon.

The shoes Virgil dared not look at scratched toward him. Hardly able to breathe, he tried to raise a hand and beg Warren, jesusgod, tried to turn his face up and get words out, while voice and throat refused to work, and as the shoes stopped before him, he all at once found strength enough to scramble to one side, to his feet, to push off, and dragged himself one step, two steps before heat and metal stabbed his back and ribs, sent him lurching though continuing to think the front door was freedom, life, salvation, if only he could make it there and push through to the other side.

He knew Warren was coming behind him, but struggled on. And it was as he reached a hand to the door that everlasting life exploded within him, that he and plate glass shattered together and he went sprawling onto the sidewalk, contriving yet to beg for mercy, thinking to offer, confess, own up in exchange for his life to every dirty little secret he had ever known. But the former chairman of a hundred committees and subcommittees, the former broker of countless deals, could manage to gurgle but a syllable before his hair was jerked back in a handful and his skull detonated, before he glimpsed, in a last shattered thought, the consequences of failing, in a crisis, to get an offer on the table.

WARREN

Once, going on the water on a Sunday in three-foot seas, heartsick over life at home, wanting, however threatening the weather, to be on his boat, to be the strongest of lobstermen, he discovered in thirty minutes' time that he could not run traps, waves were roaring and too deranged, the chopping of his boat too wild, and he was risking his life for no reason than to tempt fate and prove something to his aloof wife. It wasn't lobsters he was wanting to uncage, but himself, and it was on that same outing, turning back, that he spotted two kayakers even more foolhardy than he, caught in the fuming mess and struggling for their lives within rising and falling tons of frigid water.

They would have drowned had he not brought his boat slamming through the waves. He went at them, cut his motor to neutral and threw anchor, bellied in where one kayak kept fishtailing skyward and the other was twisting to one side and back, to one side and back, angled sixty degrees upward as he reached the passenger cavity with his grappling hook and helped bring the kayak and its half-drowned occupant back around. He worked with hands and hook, in near-misses several times of going headlong into the turmoil himself. Getting alongside that kayak most in peril, getting a grip under the man's ribs, he called up all the strength he ever possessed and lifted, pulled, dragged and tumbled vessel and passenger onto the deck of the *Lady Bee*, into a mess of spilled bait buckets, sloshing lines, gear, pots. Leaving the kayaker to himself, he engaged motor and dragged anchor, turned the *Lady Bee*'s prow to the other kayak twenty, thirty feet away—it would prove to be occupied by a woman also bereft of paddle—once more cut the motor and extended the grappling hook full-length to where she could get a grip, and holding her, pulling her, finally gripped and tumbled her onto the deck of the *Lady Bee,* too, where her partner had struggled to disengage and was on hands and knees, retching. Leaving them to gasp and spew water, Warren recovered anchor and wheel and, in time, needing an hour to smash through angry seas in what was usually a ten-minute run, returned them into the harbor and to Fort McClary where, as they let him know by shouting at him with teary laughter, they had put into the water four hours earlier. He couldn't help laughing with them, foolish children that they were; what was there to do but laugh when death had come so close? And there, hearing their shouted gratitude, feeling them squeeze his arms and shoulders, seeing them continue to weep and smile, he got them and their vessels off-loaded in waist-high water, and held at anchor as they dragged their fiberglass shells to a VW minivan where they fixed the shells on top like an upside-down catamaran—all was increasingly comical, marked with laughter and tears—saw them wave and, of all things, throw kisses as they departed, and he kept grinning as he anchored there for the storm to abate, and as he made his way home to Narrow Cove.

Those kayakers, children who had presumed the sea . . . they crossed his mind and raised unknown emotion in Warren's heart as he sat in his pickup, lost to himself. Sitting there, not knowing what to do—maybe five minutes had passed since he jerked Virgil's crispy hair and blasted a bullet through his head—it came to him that the kayakers might be grateful today, at last, to be alive, and he wished them well, wherever they were in life. Still, it was in that moment, looking to his hands and seeing he was marked with blood and matter, that a sense of wrongdoing took him over, an awareness of something being terribly wrong and being responsible. He moved the weapon from his lap to the passenger seat and, as if turning to something forgotten, reached his hands in their automatic way to start the truck's engine.

He had shot them and all was wrong. Oh, dear God, it was what he had done.

In the next moment, as he drove from the parking lot, a police cruiser came his way with flashing lights and bellowing siren. Light and sound passed beside him like a television screen. He drove on. In spite of his sense of wrongdoing he was grasping to believe that police, God, fishermen would understand, would forgive him and be on his side: Virgil and Beatrice . . . they had it coming, deserved it, it was something he should have done to them years ago.

Still there was no relief and wrongdoing kept pressing every opening he tired to occupy. What he had done was irreversible, he could see that. It was irreversible and he would not be able to argue the point with Beatrice again, would never hear her judgment of what he had done.

He continued driving slowly. His impulse wasn't to escape, or to survive, but to explain, to persuade and be understood, to be forgiven. Who wouldn't have done what he had done? Some years earlier a woman in Ogunquit had shot her husband fifteen times, emptied two clips into him, and the court had ruled it justifiable homicide for the cheating the husband had done, his flaunting in her face of cheating with younger, thinner women. Justifiable homicide.

Wrongdoing maintained its grip on Warren's heart, however, and as he drove along he began keening with uncertainty, with pain and in fear of being yet again on the wrong side of everything in life. To an imaginary judge he implored his wish only to be a husband while being cheated for thirty years! They had used him, she had said as much, had said he should have known—and he hadn't known at all! They had duped him was what they had done, when they could have let him go. And when he offered forgiveness in exchange for a touch of friendship they turned their backs on him, excluded him as if from existence. They refused to listen, even when he admitted he had brought a share of alienation on himself.

As his heart raged and he traced the marshlands curve into town, three howling/flashing police cruisers rose into view and wailed by, rising and falling like planes in an air show. He glanced to his mirror and kept knowing in his heart that everything was terribly wrong, was worse than the bodies they would find. Her precious store stained and violated with blood and glass, death and carnage. Yet again a realization came as if from on high that he would never see Beatrice again or be able to make his case. Nor might he dream, as he had so many times, of running into her in town and winning her over at last, or dream, as he had into a thousand nights, of possessing her as a woman, masturbating, fantasizing his lilac-scented, silken wife as she lay in an adjacent room behind a locked door. No, she was gone now, and terror kept coming up his throat, making him sick with what he had done.

It was not the police station but the harbor patrol headquarters where Warren pulled over to surrender. There was no last round in the Colt with which to accomplish the task, and he had not thought beforehand to use a bullet on himself, yet he was drawn to do so as he climbed from the cab and glimpsed the pistol left on the seat. He wanted badly to surrender, to explain and be understood, to be forgiven, but as he walked he felt an urge to return to the passenger side, to fish a round from the oily bag and put an end to his terrible awareness of himself and his crimes, to blow them away and leave himself in a pile of nothingness on the pavement.

He proceeded to a door next to a large two-story door, proceeded in what may have been cowardice, or retention of hope for forgiveness, however hollow he knew any hope to be. They had used and cheated him all those years, he was trying to persuade himself. Wouldn't God understand and spare him the curse of damnation? Hadn't that woman with her fifteen shots been understood and spared by God and the courts alike?

A man in a white shirt bearing small gold collar insignia sat at a dispatcher's desk and continued making notations as Warren entered and stood before him. "I shot them," Warren got out. "He was with her, all these years. God Almighty, I shot them."

The man had looked up. "You did what—you shot someone?"

"He was with her for thirty years. I tried to forgive them, but they wouldn't hear it. . . ."

The man was nearly smiling. "You shot someone? Where did this happen?"

Warren uttered their names. "She owns—Maine Authentic is the store . . . they cheated me all these years . . . they said I should have known . . . I didn't know anything."

The fireman's brow had peaked. "You shot Virgil Pound—is that what you said—you shot Virgil Pound?"

Warren was struggling against coughing or weeping. "I tried to forgive them, is what I was trying to do. I begged them to let me forgive them."

Over his shoulder the fireman was calling, "Good-man, you better get out here, Goodman! Sir, your name is—?" he added to Warren. "Are you armed, sir? You shot two people—is that what you're saying?"

Warren stood in awareness of all he had ever pos-sessed or known sinking into fathoms of darkness. His life was like a key dropped over the side, falling away too quickly to ever be recovered. Dear God, why did it have to feel so wrong?

THREE

MARIAN

She walked the beach at Seapoint in biting November air.
Days had been slipping by and she had been negotiating
the hours of her life step by step, while seeming to arrive
nowhere. The funerals and her statements to the police.
The cleanup at the store and her fractured talks with
employees and, thanks to Lori, staving off office and
management chores, recordkeeping, meeting the payroll.
Struggling with Ron and, at each step, resenting her father's
unpardonable deeds.

What he had done before her eyes seemed never to
entirely depart consciousness. Whatever his grievance he
had no right to end people's lives. His violation was so
basic, it remained with her and disrupted who she was or
would ever be.

Maine Authentic, her mother's awkward growing
child. It never stopped demanding attention, feeding,
cleaning, caretaking, adding part-time help, answering
mail, and Marian felt it would overwhelm her if she did
not find ways to control it. The baby inside her belly was
also with her each moment and was also a burden, though
one she was confident of managing—an object of new-

ness and high hopes. The store, Ron, and her father were the opposite. The problem of her father would end soon, in his inevitable dying, but she imagined herself pushed and bullied by Ron and the store for years to come if things remained unchanged.

What she wouldn't give to have her mother with her again, if only for one last day or week. She'd absorb every word and bit of advice. She'd have her mother know she appreciated all she had done for her and, as it had turned out, had given her—far more than Marian had known existed. As it was, she planned to involve her mother in the birth of her baby in the deepest possible way. One would become part of the other, and they'd all start over again. She would will it so.

Ducking her head into the sharp air, Marian acknowledged that hers had been a privileged life, but she also believed she had gained maturity in the shocking experience of recent weeks. Immaturity had fallen away like a wardrobe of old styles and colors. Her mother had given her so much (had any child in southern Maine been half as fortunate?) and on her sudden death had bequeathed more to her in properties, insurance, CDs, bank accounts than Marian had known existed. But Marian was realizing each day the relative insignificance of wealth. I guess you had to be there, she tried joking with Ron, to explain her emerging view of things, to which he replied, "Hey, babe, the bucks are real."

* * *

Well, you did have to be there, Marian thought as she ran
it through her mind once again. Having a baby was something else Ron could not incorporate and she remained
surprised at her own impulse to protect her tiny creature
back when the only world she had ever known came
crashing down around her. Her hand had gone to her baby
in primal awareness of its welfare. A year earlier she might
have dashed from the store to save her skin, but in the
crisis her hand had gone to her baby just as her heart had
gone to her parents.

If only Ron had come to her side in the aftermath,
she thought. He appeared to try, when things had been
at their worst, but seemed incapable of really doing so.
Often she pitied him, felt sorry for his shallowness, and
kept knowing all over again that she could not live with
him as the parent of their child. Separation was something
she had to make happen. She had no wish to hurt him, to
hurt anyone in any way—not now, not ever—but was
more convinced each day that she had no choice. Life had
assumed new meaning for her. You had to *know* what
you were doing, and just letting things happen was as
maddening as all else that lay unresolved around her.

Even here on the desolate beach, and as she felt she was
returning to herself, the stain of blood remained. Her
mother's blood could as well have been paint, it felt so

unremovable. Blood and the ever-clinging nightmare. She knew she was improving—while her heart would come up trembling all over again now and then, and she'd bite her knuckles to keep from crying.

Today promised to be one of her most difficult days: Her mother was buried in Kittery, Virgil was at rest in his family plot in York Village, ten miles to the north, and she was scheduled to meet with her father at the York County jail—their first meeting since the slaughter and the final meeting of their lives—for purposes of naming her power of attorney over whatever remained of family and property, including his life in terms of possible resuscitation. She did not intend to be in his presence again after today—he had been arraigned but was so near death that the formality of scheduling had been put on hold—and, like others, she regarded the promise of avoiding a trial as a small blessing. Every day since it had happened what he had done was unforgivable, and so it was today—a lens over her eyes guiding each step. There could never be an excuse for causing such loss and bloodshed. Something else could have been done. Anything but the ending of lives.

One meeting would be more than enough, and her thought—as she weighed the prospect—was to look at him without expression and say nothing unless it was to answer yes or no to a lawyer's or deputy's question. He may have been betrayed in life, but nothing under the sun gave him the right to do what he had done. That was her bottom line. Lori alone had dared say that inflicting death might at times be a person's *only* psychological option. Virgil might be held accountable for provocation, she said, for a lifetime of abusing his office for personal gain. They were issues with which Marian decided she would have to live, and while disagreeing that inflicting death might be a man's only option, she accepted Lori's honesty, believing she wanted as a friend to help her move beyond the anger she held for her father.

A figure with a dog emerged from dune grass two hundred yards away and fear seized Marian's heart. Then she saw it was a woman and her heart began parachuting back to earth. She knew she could use professional help. All at once the shock of what had happened would threaten her, and her impulse would be to get in her car and drive to a town where she wasn't known. Other times, sinking into depression, she lost respect for fear and walked wherever she wished and left doors unlocked. Or she began sobbing as if she were five years old and her mother had left her on a street in town where fire engines were screaming by.

From fearing everything to fearing nothing. From being shaken by the shriek of a gull to crossing a street between moving cars as if they did not exist. And, rarely, a thought of her father—and still another closing of her heart against him. What he had done was unforgivable.

He may have been provoked, but nothing gave anyone the right to kill. Why hadn't he moved out twenty-five years ago?

Now these new feelings of resolve: She would say and do whatever was necessary. The lessons had been horrible, the cost incalculable, still it had been an education and she was going to use it as a stepping stone to the future.

She returned over gravel and blacktop to her car. The first frost had come in the day after her mother's funeral, and along the stretch of pavement, under shedding trees, there was now the brisk air of autumn. Let the season hurry up and change, she thought. Let the leaves disappear and the snow come in great depths. Let her baby be blessed with health and let this season in her own life be replaced by memories of smiles on her mother's face, her mother serving customers and, on the side, giving her tips on getting people to like her for who she was.

Should her baby be a girl, she knew what its name would be.

Five or six men in suits and uniforms stood within the anteroom and Marian, introduced to each, filed away which were lawyers and which were county officials. She moved with the flow into a large room with a long table in the center and sunlight streaking through high screened windows on one side. The sheriff, a man with thinning beige-colored hair matching his uniform, explained what would happen. "Mrs. Slemm, your father's very sick," he said. "He's devastated over what he did and wants to say something to you by way of apology. You may listen to what he has to say, and respond, or not, as you wish. He'll be in restraints and will be brought in by deputies, so there's nothing to fear. We understand how difficult this has to be, and want only to help in any way possible. Fine so far?" he said.

Marian nodded.

"There'll be documents for you to sign as, I believe, has been explained. After the signing, your father wants to speak, but at that time, or at any time, you may terminate things by giving me a nod. Now, we don't know if you'll want physical contact with your father or not. It's up to you and you may do as you wish at the time. As a formality, we are required to sweep you with a metal detector, which I hope you don't mind. It won't be intrusive, and it's just a formality as required by law. We all set then?"

Once more Marian nodded. She perceived the elderly sheriff giving a nod, whereupon another man in uniform approached and swept over her—up one side and down the other—something like a divining rod, before stepping back.

Another nod from the sheriff followed and, across the room, a door opened and a group of uniformed deputies entered at a snail's pace. Marian looked mainly to the floor, but within her peripheral vision, as the frail figure in restraints and orange coveralls was there in the midst of uniformed guards, and as she stiffened to hold her heart in check, she perceived a pale and sick old man, as if, in the passing days, he had forgone eating and failed all the more. She took in, too, that his head was hanging as if no strength remained in his neck. And she saw a family likeness with herself in his lifelong shyness. Her nature had come more from this man, she knew, than from her mother.

The procession stopped and her father remained downcast. The sheriff articulated softly in ways that required no response from either of them, and each took a turn reaching to the table to scratch with a ballpoint beside one x and another. Though the guards and others remained at hand and there would be nothing like privacy, the sheriff said, "Mr. Hudon, if you have something to say, this is the time."

Marian sensed her father trying to lift his face, and as he did so, and against her intentions not to open to him, emotion broke in her throat like the crack of a lightbulb. She had to inhale not to sob aloud. "Marian," he uttered through tears of his own. As she forced her eyes to look up, she saw that he was unable for the moment to continue. Nor was it the restraints that had had him taking baby steps, but his health, hanging by a thread. Far from restraining him, the guards were holding him up.

He gasped, needed another moment to compose himself. "You can't forgive me," he got out. "I . . ." He appeared unable to get anything more to come forth, appeared to surrender.

When another moment passed and nothing more was said, the sheriff gave a nod and the guards appeared to lift and return him the way they had come. Marian struggled against reaching to him. In her mind's eye she saw herself emerging from napping in the pilothouse, taking a sip of coffee, and an urge was in her to undo all that had gone wrong. Still, she checked herself, restrained her heart. And when the sheriff touched her elbow, though hesitating, she moved as guided. Something within may have broken for a moment but she knew the course she had to follow, knew she had to remain strong if she was going to survive the uncertain path before her.

WARREN

Guards and kitchen staff pressed medication on him, but he lay curled on his cot in a wheezing stupor and did not look at them. They spoke in whispers, and it came to him that they were trying to help him die. It was peace they were trying to grant him, and their kindness was a mystery to him. If he had a wish, it was to be relieved of life and of himself as soon as possible. He had proved unworthy of being helped or of being remembered. Obstacles had been placed before him and he had proven himself unworthy as a human being.

* * *

"These pills will help," someone said close by.

"It gets bad, you let us know," the voice said another time.

A doctor, upon a cursory examination, whispered, "Morphine will help, Mr. Hudon, but it can't be prescribed until they move you to the hospital—which should happen soon. The paperwork's in."

Warren asked for nothing, said nothing, continued to suffer from faltering perception, and wanted only to be gone from awareness of the failure his life had been, gone from himself and the crimes he had committed. The doctor sat on the side of his cot and spoke, in a near-whisper, of last-minute intervention, aggressive procedures, unnecessary pain. He spoke of one's inner life, and Warren believed the doctor knew what he was talking about. Warren regretted that his inner life did not deserve to know peace and tried to indicate no to life being extended. The doctor leaned close. "It'll be better on the other side," he whispered, and Warren gave no sign unless it was to shift his pupils, perhaps to blink his eyes.

Being awake was to be in pain in his conscience, and dozing was barely different. Moments awake passed like dirty ice melting in March. He had no way of refusing medications, which paved over the gravel in his throat and let him escape into semiconsciousness. His ability to breathe had diminished to one wheezing breath, then another, and running out of breath was a promise waiting at the end, a sliding into many-colored radiance. *Take me unto Thee, O Lord,* he prayed in one moment, while feeling undeserving even of the mysterious joy of death.

Wakefulness persisted. His actions with the heavy Colt Python hovered like hallucinations and made his mind swirl with anxiety. He could not speak or give any sign and lay half comatose. Persons clanged into the cell, pressed tablets and a tiny paper cup of water between his lips, clanged out, slid needles into his arm. Still he saw himself firing into Beatrice, grabbing Virgil's hair, firing into his skull.

"Your move to the hospital is in the works," a familiar voice whispered.

Then the voice said experimental drugs were available, CPR could be used, asked if he wouldn't change his mind. Warren wanted only to disappear. Nor did he wish to lie in the ground next to Beatrice, if any such possibility remained, though no one had asked and he had neither strength nor voice enough to object. His ploy to lie beside her repulsed him in his self-abasement, while he retained no capacity for asking to be cast into the sea and lost to awareness once and for all.

When daylight in the high windows gave way to evening, shadows spread over him and offered a cover within which to lie concealed. All his life he had taken pleasure in day breaking from the ocean and now it was twilight that afforded pleasure—until fluorescent lights crackled with sudden wavering glare, shattering the early and peaceful close of day. Fluorescent lights and sounds of television suggested eternal hell.

For moments in the dying afternoon, seeing shapes within shadows, there came feelings of serenity. The sun lowering beneath the horizon and darkness following was a work of art in nature he had rarely regarded before seeing it violated here by milk-colored and hissing fluorescent lights. Color, departing the sky, gave way to shadows and shapes of immortality: Closing of day on the harbor was a gift he had been too mortal to appreciate. The harbor at dusk, lights wavering from shore, was all he wanted his eyes ever to see again.

It came to him in darkness that in killing Beatrice he had killed himself, had killed in her what she had allowed him, from their earliest days together, to be. It wasn't justifiable homicide at all, but murder, he admitted to his conscience. From the moment of clearing his boat and hefting the Python his heart had known what it wanted to do. From that moment on God had known it wasn't forgiveness he was seeking but vengeance. And God was the judge before him now.

* * *

The voice came again. *"Now and at the hour of our death, may the Lord bless thee and be with thee,"* it said. Then it said, *"Amen."*

So it was that when death came for Warren Hudon, television sounds hovered above his thin perception. A ballplayer loped bases, entering an increasing roar while fluorescent lights buzzed overall. Heaven and hell. Like a trap sliding from his boat and being left behind, he began cascading away from awareness. Buzzing persisted while his breath missed one beat and another, rattled faintly, disappeared into watery darkness.

MARIAN

Neither Ron nor the store would leave her alone. Ron was like a fist holding the back of her neck. The more she thought of him the more certain she was in her judgment, and she kept looking for an excuse or occasion to end their hopeless marriage. Once in a while he would say or do something, or she would have a tender thought of him from the past, or of the baby being *their* product, and uncertainty over breaking up would travel her veins like a lyric from a song. Then he would say or do something— anything—and certainty would once more take charge of the center of her skull. She'd have a child by him—she had no choice—but would not raise a child with him.

Getting free of him was a problem she had to solve, for she knew well the folly of staying in a bad marriage.

The store was more complicated. As much as it was a burden, it was like a difficult research project in which she was hopelessly behind. Simply thinking of its demands and problems raised panic in her, made her want to cash it all in and run away to something clear and simple. Then she knew she could not run away, for it would be cowardice of the worst kind, defeat for which neither she nor her mother would ever be able to forgive her. She might get out of retail, in time, but not in the wake of her mother's death and not as an act of cowardice. She could not just give up. She had to get a handle on the store and keep it from careening off-track. She had no choice but to fill her mother's shoes. Anything less would haunt her forever.

Nor was the store without hope or rewards, she'd have to admit. As often as she grew weary of the hours and pressure, of the tedium of chores, she relished the people and the talk, the fun of a busy morning and a pleasure in satisfying customers, in feeling quiet fulfillment at the end of a long day of working hard and getting things accomplished, if they had to do with mastering the accounts payable program or staying late to clean shelves and polish a hundred goblets. At times, having lunch with Lori and being moved to tears by her friendship, being visited and offered support by neighboring merchants, just depositing receipts late at night, satisfaction would fill her on driving home and at bedtime premature urges to be back on the job, working with friends, picking up where they left off, would race through her confused heart.

Then next season's inventory, holiday help, tax payments and quarterly statements would return her to near panic and she'd long all over again for a simple life. Running a business was a hundred problems at once, and however petty some of them seemed to be, at times she feared she was incapable of handling one or two. How had her mother pulled it off and maintained her sanity and niceness? Had she been stronger than Marian had known? Craftier? More versatile? More gifted than her daughter?

Throughout all, Marian had yet to determine where to bury the man who was her father. Their family plot, a block of four, had been purchased years ago and three of the spaces remained available. The first question she faced, the morning after the call reporting his death, was in having a service and, if so, what kind of service? He had no relatives to be invited, though he did have acquaintances in the area, fishermen friends who belonged to the Co-op and who, no matter recent events, might choose to attend.

Would she herself attend?

Her impulse was to say no to both. There was no need to provide a service and if one were offered there was no need for her to be present. But as hours slipped by and she gained added distance, she wondered if she did not owe her father a service for his better years and would regret, later, not having provided one. It would not be a gesture of forgiveness, not on her part, but she determined that offering a small ceremony, if only for his friends, would be a taking of the high road. And she could quietly attend, if only as a family witness.

Would such a service help put the mess behind her? She believed it would, then would swing back to not wishing to honor or acknowledge in any way the man who had ended her mother's life in cold blood. She could not forgive that which might never be forgiven. He deserved nothing. Her resolve may have slipped for a moment at the jail but she continued to believe she had to hold firm, or surrender to what was unacceptable.

When a solution came to her it was hardly a surprise. Weeks after the shootings and on the day after her father's death, driving to the cemetery to where her mother's plot had yet to be marked by a headstone, the solution was obvious: She would cast her father's ashes out to sea, where he had spent most of his life. She would not bury him next to her mother but have him cremated. She sensed at once that the decision was appropriate. Burying her father next to her mother was out of the question, for even in death he posed a threat.

She told the funeral director she would like a brief service at St. Joseph's, and that she wanted her father to be cremated, and would cast his ashes out to sea. So it was that she declined an urn and agreed to be in receipt, in time, of a container whose contents she might dispose of when and where she wished. They used a cardboard container with a screw-on lid, the man explained, and she would be contacted when it was ready to be picked up.

Perhaps two dozen persons congregated in the chapel at the parish in Kittery. Marian dressed in black and wore a veil and, with Ron at her side, they were the last to enter— the priest awaited their arrival before beginning—and, according to protocol, the first to leave. Returning home after the service, and while Ron took the rest of the day off, Marian left for the store to work into the evening. Her motive was to flush the morning's events and, if hardly admitting it to herself, to be away from Ron.

At the store there were ongoing demands for introducing the Thomaston line. On this day it was less worrisome to Marian to be *in* the store than away—fewer things threatened to escape control when she was there—and she also knew she was growing less intimidated in areas of management if she got herself involved. She telephoned Janet Derocher, telephoned her mother's computer tutor to confirm bookkeeping entries, telephoned McInnes Business College to ask still more questions having to do with the Thomaston sequence and her mother's plan to introduce the line before Christmas. The inmates' handicraft

had been her mother's pet project and Marian feared she
wasn't carrying it off on time or as her mother would have
liked. A handful of weeks and a ticking clock—yet another realization of the number of tasks her mother had
looked after herself.

Marian tried every day to recall how her mother
handled things. On occasions of successfully untangling
not just a problem but a procedure, and imagining her
mother performing the same task, tears might fill her eyes:
signing where her mother had signed, transferring funds,
having someone on the phone tell her she sounded just
like her mother and wishing her good luck. Not rarely,
sitting at her mother's desk and aware of the child she
might touch by sliding a hand over her belly, Marian let
her emotions run as they might. Resting her face in her
hand, resting her head on her arm, she would evoke her
mother and address words to her. *I'm getting there, I'm
doing my best,* she liked to say. *I can't believe how much
I miss you,* she liked to say. *There are times when this place
drives me crazy and I don't know if I can deal with it,* she
also liked to say.

That her mother and child could be *with* her in the
quiet office was testimony to something more than money
being her legacy. The three of them, they belonged to and
had each other. The bucks were real but next to the people
with whom one might be interwoven, body and soul, the
bucks were mere pieces of paper.

* * *

The media had not hounded her, except at a distance. Images and voices of television had surrounded everything for days and conveyed a sense of a many-lighted space station hovering overhead. At her mother's funeral there were antennas, photographers, a loose mob of onlookers they drew with them, staring and flashing all around. They were not in her face with their cameras nor were they discreet. The details of news reports were often threatening and she came to rarely read or watch anything through to its end. All she could think was that news wasn't so entertaining when the people belonged to you, that it was "weird" to see the ways in which things were distorted. Television commentators seemed always in a rush to move to a commercial and their reports sounded like parodies:

"A story going around up in Maine . . ."

"Here's one our viewers may not have heard . . ."

"In domestic abuse, silence may be the real enemy . . ."

Domestic abuse was mentioned several times as the subject and some reports had it that a jealous husband had killed his wife for refusing to meet him for lunch. Marian tried to remain unaffected, yet wished that at least one eloquent voice would say it had been a thirty-year affair and nothing about it had been domestic. A love triangle, the call to a woman of a powerful man; that had the been the age-old dilemma, and also the instance of domestic abuse, if not the kind the reporters had in mind.

One evening she heard, ". . . reported to be near death in a Down East jail cell is the lobsterman who contracted cancer and in retaliation killed his wife and her business partner . . ." and she began at once to laugh and weep, then only to weep as she made her way from the room. Cancer might be cured in time, she thought, but there would be no such luck in the ailments of love and betrayal.

Days later there came an evening when she and Ron were cleaning up after dinner, when Ron lost his cool—again— and she heard herself say to him, "Ron, listen, I'd like you to move out of here, tonight—in a separation that will lead to divorce."

Just like that the words were out. His first response was to smirk—a relief to her, because she had feared he might explode. Dinner was over, she would be going to the store again to work late—Thomaston products continued to arrive and she needed to get them inventoried, needed, against all odds, to initiate a plan for presenting the new line—and there were the words that had been playing in her mind for weeks. From smirking, Ron was gurgling as if trying to laugh, though a moment earlier intense anger had gripped his face. "You what?" he said.

Putting in blocks of time at the store, Marian had been making telephone inquiries into legalities of separation, property settlement, child custody, and divorce. Her plan had been to present a proposal to Ron, in writing or maybe in a sit-down negotiation at the kitchen table; then, a moment ago, dropping a fork as he rose from the table, kicking it violently over the floor, he offered the opening and now the words hung between them like icicles. "You heard what I said—do I have to say it again?"

"Yeah, right, like I'm moving out," he said.

"Ron, I'm not joking."

He kept gazing, appearing uncertain how to respond. In her eyes he had reverted months ago to being an adolescent and so he appeared to her now: a brash high school boy confronted with a force beyond his range. "I've thought about this for a long time," she said. "I don't want to hurt you."

"You know, I think you're serious," he said as if to mock.

"Ron, I'm serious."

"What brought this on?"

"Everything."

"There's someone else?"

This time she did the smirking, though genuinely so. "I'm three months pregnant, grow up," she said.

He stared. "You really are serious, aren't you?"

"I said I was."

"What about the baby?" he said, as if concerned.

"I'll take care of the baby. I won't be asking for child support, or alimony."

"As if I'd pay either one. With what?"

However uncertain she was of the terrain before her, Marian's impulse was to push forward and get her cards played. "I'll be giving you a settlement—as a way of discharging claims," she said.

He laughed. "You got the lingo down," he said.

"Nothing's ever going to work for us, that's what we need to recognize. We were finished as a couple a long time ago."

He looked at her, stared as if waiting for instructions.

"This can be congenial or not, I don't care," she said. "I'd like you to move out, and if you won't, I will. I'm prepared to make a cash settlement, to cover everything. I'll assume debts, including all child-rearing expenses, the mortgage, everything else. You make me do the moving, you choose to make it messy—I won't give you a thing and I'll fight you every step of the way. And I'll win, believe me."

He stared another moment before saying, "You had all that memorized, didn't you."

She gave no reply, and he said, "What kind of cash settlement?"

"Well, fifty thousand dollars," Marian said. "Which you can pay to a lawyer or keep for yourself."

He kept staring at her. "You're too much," he said. "How long you been planning all this?"

Knowing she had him where she wanted him, Marian had no intention of allowing an opening. "I've talked to some people and they say that amount is fair," she said. "You have to say if you're willing to accept the terms."

"Hey, doesn't sound bad to me." Again, he forced a grin, and she imagined him already spending the money in his mind.

"We owe over ninety thousand on the house, there's not much equity, and if you choose to act in a juvenile way, I'll fight it, and you'll pay through the nose for years. I've checked it out—I know what I'm talking about. I need to know if you'll accept, or if you're going to hire a lawyer who will say you should have accepted the terms a long time ago and will keep half the money himself."

Ron snickered, but then he said, "What about the baby having a father?" and a hitch in his voice sent a faint tremor through her heart.

"I'll take care of the baby."

"I meant about custody and visiting," he said.

Again he was trying to smirk, but she knew he was terrified and thought he was going to cry. "I'll retain custody and I'll allow visits," she said. "There won't be any question about custody. You don't want it anyway, so don't say something you don't mean. That kind of talk is over, it is for me."

His eyes had glossed over, if but slightly, while he appeared to be trying yet to smirk and laugh for cover. This right now is the hard part, Marian told herself, urging herself to hold firm. Whatever the hurt, whatever any desire to stop it or make it go away, she had to look to days ahead. "It's time to grow up," she added, nearly giving way to tears of her own.

A moment passed. She thought Ron was holding silent in awareness of his voice breaking should he try to speak. Then he said, "How do I know that amount is fair?" and she felt relief, vindication, hope, disappointment. If he believed money was the bottom line, she was all the more certain he deserved to be cut off and left behind.

"The store's worth money but I'll have debts and a child to raise. It's fair. You don't want this to come down to fighting over money." This time she did the staring, into his cornered eyes.

"Think about it," she said as he remained silent. "I won't be changing the offer, only if you refuse to cooperate. Pack your stuff and leave. Go stay with Greg. Call me at the store tomorrow and I'll get papers drawn up. I'll get the money together and get it to you as soon as I can. Just think, you can buy yourself a new Transam."

"Screw you," he said.

"Whatever. Just say if you accept the offer."

"Hey, give me an hour and I'm outta here." His words were off-key and he angled his chin as if, yet again, to grin and laugh.

Marian did the blinking, such as it was. Closing the lapels of her coat, she said, "I'll talk to a lawyer. Ron, I'm sorry," she added.

* * *

She crossed to her car in the frosty air. From kicked fork to the end, hardly ten minutes had passed. As she settled behind the wheel, and paused, it came to her that she was into an out-of-body experience and had to return to earth. She started the engine. What to do? Only as she looked over her shoulder did tears of fear, uncertainty, heartache over hurting Ron, blur her eyes. She held there, attempted to keep her eyes open and blinked again.

She instructed herself to see that this was the climax of the hardest part. In an hour, when he had left, when she had caught her breath, the worst would be over. Later, when she returned and the house was empty, there would be pain and doubt, but nothing like this. She had gotten the words out! That was the thing to focus on. Now she had only to stay her course and keep looking ahead until six months, nine months, a year had passed, until her baby was with her and the store was under control. As several people had remarked, her life remained before her.

Backing out, rolling away, Marian began missing her mother. Who else to turn to in a moment like this? However corny it had been at times to admit it, her mother had been her best friend. Her pal at work, with winks, averted eyes to the ceiling when someone was jabbering and boring everyone to tears. Laughter so shared they might at times have been the same person. The one friend to whom, phone wedged to her ear and mixing bowl in hand, she might describe every detail of what she was fixing for Sunday dinner. What a godsend it would be to be able to speak to her now.

But her mother was gone and it was time to face up and move on, Marian thought as she came to a dark stop sign and turned left onto the secondary road that led to the highway. Strive to fill her shoes. Go ahead and be a businesswoman, and do it right, she thought. What other choice did she have?

She drove on, and to keep her vision clear for the road, avoided wiping her filmed-over eyes. The little Miata, her graduation gift from Virgil and her mother, was five years old now, and as she traced its headlights into darkness she saw that it was time to trade it in, to buy something new and different. Not her mother's car—awaiting disposition in a Portsmouth garage—but something her mother would like, she thought. Something safe for her baby, and safe on nights like these when she drove to that warmth of unpacking and shelving that was becoming her refuge. Something to see her safely home when she was fulfilled with work and, as she had come to realize, would be preoccupied with ongoing ideas on the return drive into country darkness. Maybe a new Chrysler, Marian thought as she turned south onto the I-95 ramp.

Why not? Maybe her mother had had a point.

* * *

On the day of the opening Marian decided, spontaneously, to dispose of her father's ashes. She was dressed and ready to leave the house, and the day appeared reasonable for both events. The container rested on a shelf in the entryway to the kitchen—her eyes took it in often—and it came to her that this was the perfect day. Ron, she had heard, was already running around, her ill-will toward her father had settled, the wind velocity was low this morning, and it was a step she had been wanting to put behind her. Whatever the direction of the tide, the ashes would touch upon the water and disappear. While she was receiving customers and guests coming to see the new line the ashes would wash throughout the harbor and out to sea. In the store there would be a sense in the air, however privately, of life going on.

The summer when she served as first mate on his boat her father had made her aware of the channel winding down the center of the harbor, and it was where she wished to dispose of his ashes. "We're in the channel," he liked to remark when they returned from the near expanse of ocean, and there was always a sense of entering a safe passageway, a depth of water to follow under the Route 1 bridge to the Co-op and the safety of land where the surface underfoot was no longer fluid with uncertainty. Deposited into the channel, the ashes would return her father to the world he had loved, and it was a degree of forgiveness she was ready to grant. As for death being his only option, she had come around to feeling sympathy for his frustration as a husband, but not for his actions. Down through his life, other choices had been available. He had failed to act.

Moves planned, Marian drove to the marina on the Maine side of the bridge. From there, leaving her car, she walked through sharp sunlit air onto the span of the old green superstructure with its metal railings and wooden plank walkways. A lobster boat was passing beneath the bridge, going out, and against her better judgment she took a moment to watch it recede. It was a one-man boat, its noise as steady as a single-engine plane. The lone occupant at the wheel held her eye. All was familiar, and she knew that in letting her father go she was also letting him remain.

Breeze and tide were outgoing, the water that had visited the harbor washing back into the ocean. Through wind blurring her eyes, she checked pilings thirty feet below and reconfirmed the tidal flow. The air, a light breeze to fishermen, remained broad and even. She took in a breath, and sensed the sea rising like a living creature to receive what she had to offer.